P9-DGB-950

Jennifer couldn't believe how smug Claudia was being. What made her think she was going to win? There were lots of other couples at North Ridge High. Maybe one of them would be voted Most Romantic. There was no guarantee that Claudia and Chase were going to win. If they made the final cut, they were going to be stiff competition. But that didn't mean they were the most romantic. And it didn't mean they deserved to win!

Listening to Claudia go on and on, Jennifer wanted nothing more than to knock her down a few pegs. She couldn't stand listening to her anymore! Claudia was *so* sure that she and Chase were going to win.

Before Jennifer could stop herself, the words came tumbling out of her mouth.

"I wouldn't be too sure about winning," she said.

Also by Sabrina James

Secret Santa

Unit #9
Glenn Raymond School

SABRINA JAMES

♡♡♡♡♡ Point ♡♡♡♡♡

Copyright © 2009 by John Scognamiglio

All rights reserved. Published by Point, an imprint of Scholastic Inc., *Publishers since 1920*. SCHOLASTIC, POINT, and associated logos are trademarks and/or registered trademarks of Scholastic Inc.

No part of this publication may be reproduced, stored in a retrieval system, or transmitted in any form or by any means, electronic, mechanical, photocopying, recording, or otherwise, without written permission of the publisher. For information regarding permission, write to Scholastic Inc., Attention: Permissions Department, 557 Broadway, New York, NY 10012.

Library of Congress Cataloging-in-Publication Data

James, Sabrina.
Be mine / by Sabrina James.—1st ed.
p. cm.
Summary: When she brags that she is entering the competition of the most romantic couple for the Valentine's Day Dance, Jennifer has only one problem—she needs a boyfriend.
ISBN-13: 978-0-545-09739-0 (alk. paper)
ISBN-10: 0-545-09739-8 (alk. paper)
[1. Dating (Social customs)—Fiction. 2. Valentine's Day—Fiction. 3. High schools—Fiction. 4. Schools—Fiction. 5. Friendship—Fiction.] I. Title.
PZ7J154365Be 2009
[Fic]—dc22
2008021528

12 11 10 9 8 7 6 5 4 3 2 1 9 10 11 12 13 14/0

Printed in the U.S.A.
First edition, January 2009
Text design by Steve Scott
Text type set in Plantin

Acknowledgments

Special thanks to my terrific editors, Abigail McAden and Morgan Matson, who allowed me to pay another visit to North Ridge High! Thanks, too, to my agent, Evan Marshall.

Thanks also to all the readers who emailed to tell me how much they enjoyed Secret Santa. I hope you all love this book just as much!

Memo

To: The Students of North Ridge High
From: Principal Seymour Hicks
Date: Wednesday, February 6
Subject: Valentine's Day!

Attention all couples! Do you think you and your sweetheart are the most romantic couple at North Ridge High? If you do, we want to know!

Tell us in an essay of five hundred words or less submitted no later than this Friday. Over the weekend, the essays will be read by myself and three other members of the faculty. On Monday, we'll reveal which five couples will be chosen to compete as Most Romantic. Those couples will have until Valentine's Day to show their classmates why they should be voted Most Romantic.

The winning couple will be announced at next Thursday's Valentine's Day dance and will receive an evening for two in New York City, complete with a chauffeur-driven limousine, dinner, and tickets to a Broadway show. Runners-up will receive a five-pound box of chocolate.

Happy Valentine's Day!

Chapter One

"I hate Valentine's Day!" seventeen-year-old Jennifer Harris exclaimed.

Jennifer's best friend, Violet Wagner, stared at her over the black rims of her cat-eye-shaped glasses. "I thought you only hated Christmas. Now you've added Valentine's Day to the list."

"Have you seen this?" Jennifer waved at Violet the memo she had found inside her locker that morning. "Have you?"

"Uh, no," Violet said, taking off her pink parka and unwrapping the long pink scarf wrapped around her neck. "I just got here and I'm *still* freezing. It's *so* cold outside. I feel like a Popsicle! They say we might get a snowstorm this weekend." Violet's blue eyes glittered with excitement. "Wouldn't it be cool if it lasted until Monday and we got a snow day?"

shoving the
" she insisted
oved hands.
st there was
ber and now
able?"
ien handed it
d what all the

feel inferior

ing her parka
ig classes. As
floated to the
ks is conspir-
ve boyfriends

grumbled.
didn't have
the way some
Secret Santa

oyfriends for
Secret Santa
-pack of Wint

minty-fresh

breath. You should be flattered! Obviously, he was hoping for a kiss! It's not too late. I bet he'd let you give him one for Valentine's Day."

Jennifer scowled. "He didn't get one then and he's not getting one now. And don't mention that day to me!"

Jennifer had always hated Valentine's Day. The reason was that she'd never had a boyfriend on that day. Sure, she'd gone on a number of dates since junior high, but she had never had a long-term boyfriend the way some of the other girls in her class had. Every Valentine's Day she would get to see those girls get boxes of candy and bouquets of flowers and hear about their Valentine's Day dates. When was she going to have her first real Valentine's Day?

"You know I'm happy to be your date for Valentine's Day," Violet said as she picked up the memo and stuck it into her oversized shoulder bag. She closed her locker and started walking down the hall with Jennifer. "We can rent some chick flicks and pretend we're the ones falling in love."

"Uh-uh. No way," Jennifer said with determination. "We're not going to be couch potatoes this year. We're going to the Valentine's Day dance."

A look of panic washed over Violet's face. "Alone?"

guys do it. It's the perfect
"
e and shook her head,
own curls bobbing. "No,

getting stuck with the

We're going to be left-

n't meet someone? Then
humiliating is that! And
e going to be surrounded
ho get to *flaunt* the fact
e while the rest of us are
ice started to rise. "Do
their baby talk? Do you
m slow-dancing and kiss-
way holding hands? Why
special day and we don't?

triumphantly exclaimed.
ne way as me!"
olet grumbled. "I hate
hate seeing all those cute
store windows, knowing

that I'm not going to get one. I hate going into card stores and seeing all those pink and red envelopes, knowing I'm not going to find one in my mailbox. I hate going into stores, smelling all that delicious chocolate and knowing I'm going to buy a box of it when it's marked fifty percent off the next day instead of having a guy give it to me. And I especially hate that I'm not going to have my own special someone to cuddle up with on February fourteenth. Who's going to walk me to my front door after our Valentine's Day date and kiss me like I've never been kissed before because he has feelings for me and only me." Violet wrinkled her noses at Jennifer. "How do you *always* get me to confess my deep dark secrets?"

"Easy," Jennifer said, tossing her arm around Violet's shoulders and giving her a hug. "Best friends know each other inside and out."

Jennifer and Violet had been best friends since third grade. They had bonded when they both hadn't been invited to Claudia Monroe's ninth birthday party. Claudia was the richest girl in their class and made sure everyone knew it. Whatever she wanted, her parents bought for her, so she was always the first to have the latest "hot" item. She had an inground swimming pool *inside* her house and was always having pool parties, even in the winter. During the summer and on school breaks, she and her family traveled the world and sometimes Claudia would get to bring along a friend or two. All expenses paid, of course. Everyone wanted to be her friend.

But Jennifer didn't.

Jennifer didn't like Claudia because she was a fake. She was trying to buy friendship with all her money, Jennifer thought, and she didn't like the fact that Claudia thought she was better than everyone else. The fact that she was rich made her think she could do and say whatever she wanted.

She was a spoiled brat.

Jennifer suspected that Claudia knew she didn't like her. Jennifer didn't advertise her feelings — she wasn't stupid! — but she never hung out with Claudia and her friends at lunch or after school. Unlike other girls in her class, she never sucked up to Claudia, asking her if she wanted to do homework together or if she wanted to hang out.

But Violet had wanted to be friends with Claudia.

That year, Violet was the new girl in their

class. She and her family had moved to North Ridge over the summer. She was quiet and studious and loved to read — she always had her nose buried in a book. From the way Violet's eyes would always follow Claudia's every move, Jennifer could see Violet wanted to be friends with Claudia, but Claudia didn't want to be friends with Violet. Often, Jennifer would hear Claudia call Violet a nerd behind her back. And she would do it in a voice loud enough for Violet to hear. But Violet never said anything. Maybe she was hoping if she didn't, she would pass some sort of test with Claudia and become her friend. But Claudia still ignored Violet and snubbed her every chance she got.

The way Claudia treated Violet made Jennifer mad. So what if Violet liked to read and she was the smartest girl in their class? That didn't mean she deserved to be laughed at. Jennifer knew there was a reason behind Claudia's actions. Until Violet arrived, Claudia had been the smartest girl in their class.

Now she wasn't.

Violet was.

And Claudia didn't like it.

So she decided to teach Violet a lesson.

ɔeen talking about
party and how her
: a carnival in their
going to be a booth
el apples, but there
r cars, a merry-go-
gician. Claudia had
r invitations out at
was invited. Except
didn't care, but she
s were hurt. When
vasn't being invited,
g a nerd-free party.
lower lip started to
ne girls' bathroom.
nd could hear sob-
v seconds and then
et a tissue to wipe

rty?" Jennifer told
our own!"
s mother had made
nt the day listening
s, watching DVDs,
udia. They talked
: their favorite TV

shows, movie stars, and musicians, and discovered how much they had in common. After that, they were joined at the hip.

"Are you ready for Mr. Seliski's test today?" Violet asked, cutting into Jennifer's thoughts.

"I don't know why we have to take Anatomy and Physiology. It's not like I'm planning to become a doctor."

"You didn't want to take Physics, remember?"

"Well, duh! I almost failed Chemistry. There was no way I was taking another hard science class. I thought Seliski's class would be a breeze. Instead, we're constantly cutting things up. Blech!"

"It'll look good on your transcript," Violet said.

"If I hear the word *transcript* one more time, I'm going to scream!" Jennifer exclaimed. "My guidance counselor keeps telling me I need to do more extracurricular activities, but how can I when I have a part-time job? College isn't going to pay for itself. I need to start saving."

"I'm sure you're going to win a scholarship. With the exception of Chemistry last year, your grades are pretty good."

Jennifer crossed her fingers. "Let's hope!"

When Jennifer and Violet got to Mr. Seliski's door, they found it was locked.

"I guess he's running late this morning," Violet said.

Jennifer didn't answer. She was too busy listening to Claudia Monroe, who was a few feet away and leaning against a locker. As always, she had Eden Atkins and Natalie Bauer, her two best friends, by her side. Jennifer actually liked Eden and Natalie although she couldn't understand why they were friends with Claudia. Neither one of them could be branded a Mean Girl the way Claudia was. Yet all three of them had been friends since freshman year.

"I should tell Principal Hicks to not even bother reading all those other essays," Claudia said. "Chase and I are going to win. Can you think of any other couple at North Ridge High that's more romantic than us?"

Jennifer wanted to roll her eyes. If Claudia was a Mean Girl, then Chase was her Dumb Jock accessory. He was barely passing his classes but managed to skate by because he was on North Ridge High's football, basketball, and baseball teams. True, they had been dating since freshman year, but that didn't mean they were romantic. Mean girls always dated jocks. It was a high school rule. Of course, it didn't hurt that Chase was hunkalicious. He was over six feet tall and buff, with buzzed brown hair and dark blue eyes.

"I wonder if there are going to be crowns. Like at prom. Do you think we'll get crowned?" Claudia asked. She didn't wait for Eden and Natalie to answer. "There have to be crowns! Otherwise how else are we going to stand out? I'm going to have to make sure I have the perfect dress and it *has to* be pink. Pink for Valentine's Day!"

Jennifer couldn't believe how smug Claudia was being. What made her think she was going to win? There were lots of other couples at North Ridge High. Maybe one of them would be voted Most Romantic. There was no guarantee that Claudia and Chase were going to win. Of course, this *was* high school and the popular crowd *always* ruled. Claudia and Chase had *tons* of friends. If they made the final cut, they were going to be stiff competition. But that didn't mean they were the most romantic. And it didn't mean they deserved to win!

Listening to Claudia go on and on, Jennifer

wanted nothing more than to knock her down a few pegs. She couldn't stand listening to her anymore! Claudia was *so* sure that she and Chase were going to win.

Before Jennifer could stop herself, the words came tumbling out of her mouth.

"I wouldn't be too sure about winning," she said.

Claudia looked away from Eden and Natalie, staring at Jennifer with a bored expression. "And why's that?"

"Because you're going to have some competition."

"From who?"

"Me and my boyfriend."

Claudia's green eyes widened and she stared at Jennifer in disbelief. "Boyfriend? *You* have a boyfriend?"

"Why do you find that so hard to believe?" Jennifer demanded, trying hard not to sound hostile. She didn't want Claudia to know that her comment bugged her.

Claudia shrugged and tossed her short cap of blonde hair. "You've always been more of a serial dater. You know. One guy one week. Another guy another week."

"I just hadn't found the right guy."

Claudia folded her arms over the front of her cashmere sweater. Jennifer knew it was cashmere because the department store where she worked part-time sold them. They were *super* expensive. Even with the after-Christmas markdown and her store discount, she still wasn't able to afford to buy one. But Claudia had the exact same sweater in three different colors. "But now you have?"

"That's right. I have. I've been seeing someone since New Year's Eve. We met at a party. It was *so* romantic. The clock struck midnight and we were both standing next to each other and he asked if he could give me my first kiss of the new year. How could I say no?"

"Why haven't I seen the two of you together?" Claudia asked.

"We've been keeping things low-key," Jennifer said, wondering if Claudia was buying any of what she was saying. She tried to keep track of everything she'd said so far. Without a doubt, Claudia would remember every single word of this conversation and then try to trip Jennifer up at another time.

The bell for first class rang and Claudia stepped away from the locker she was leaning against. "I'm glad you've found someone. It's about time! I'm giving a party on Saturday night. Why don't you come?"

It was the first time Jennifer had ever been invited to one of Claudia's parties. She couldn't believe it.

"Thanks for the invite," she said, not wanting to appear rude.

"So you'll come?"

Jennifer shrugged and answered without thinking. "Sure. Why not?"

Claudia smiled and as her smile grew, Jennifer realized she'd just made a mistake. A big one. Claudia had set a trap and she'd unknowingly stepped right into it. Instantly, her stomach dropped and butterflies began dancing around. The look of glee on Claudia's face was similar to that of a cat who had cornered a mouse and was getting ready to pounce.

"Don't forget to bring your boyfriend," Claudia added.

"B-b-bring my boyfriend?" Jennifer said.

"That's right. You're a couple, aren't you?"

"Yes."

"You're not going to leave him home alone on a Saturday night. *Everyone* can meet him!"

"Everyone?" Jennifer gasped.

"You know how big my parties can be! Most of North Ridge High will be there." Claudia's green eyes narrowed and Jennifer felt like she was being examined under a microscope. "Your boyfriend will be able to come, won't he?"

"Of course!"

Claudia smiled smugly. "Good! I can't wait to meet him."

As soon as Claudia disappeared around the corner for her first class, with Eden and Natalie right behind her, Violet grabbed Jennifer by the arm, shaking her.

"Are you crazy?" Violet asked, keeping her voice low so no one could overhear her. "Have you lost your mind? What are you doing? You don't have a boyfriend!"

Jennifer's racing heart slowed down. The panic was subsiding and she was starting to think rationally again.

"Not yet, I don't," Jennifer said with determination. "But I will."

"By Saturday night?" Violet asked in disbelief.

"By Saturday night," Jennifer vowed.

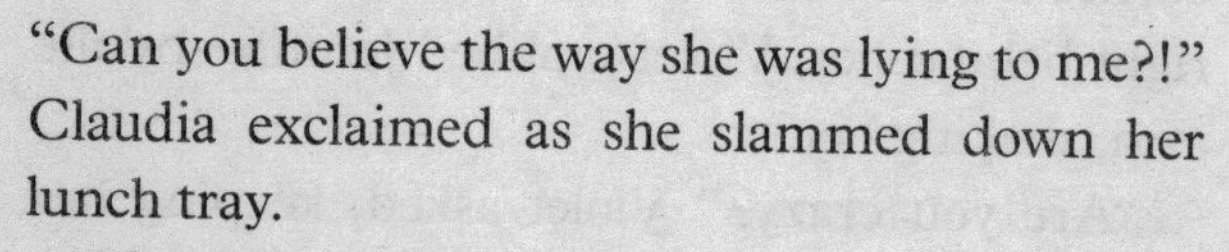

Chapter Two

"Can you believe the way she was lying to me?!" Claudia exclaimed as she slammed down her lunch tray.

Natalie slid into the seat next to Claudia, while Eden took the seat across from them. Natalie knew Claudia didn't expect an answer. Ever since seeing Jennifer that morning, Claudia had been ranting and raving between classes. And now she had the whole lunch period to do the same.

Usually when Claudia ranted, Natalie just listened. But she was tired of this conversation and dared to ask a question. "How do you know she was lying?"

Claudia looked up from the salad she was drizzling with honey mustard dressing. "Come on! Don't tell me you bought her story? It was so obvious that she was making it up on the spot."

"Why would she do that?" Eden asked as she opened a container of milk and popped a straw into it.

"She's jealous," Claudia said smugly. "She's always been jealous of me. It goes all the way back to grade school."

Natalie didn't know what to say to that. She had always seen Jennifer as being *nice*. She didn't seem like the kind of girl who would be jealous of someone else. But maybe Claudia was right. After all, she'd only been friends with Claudia since freshman year and Claudia had known Jennifer a lot longer than she had. And it really wasn't like she *knew* Jennifer. Over the years they'd had some classes together and they sometimes crossed paths when they were outside school, but it wasn't like they were *friends* the way she was with Claudia and Eden. They hung out with their group, and Jennifer hung out with hers.

Sometimes there were days when Natalie still couldn't believe she was friends with Claudia and Eden. Natalie was considered one of the most popular girls at North Ridge High and it

den had asked her
irst day of school

Claudia and Eden
have lunch with
talie and not the
rs ago.
ut her life before
starting classes at

the same person.

n fat.
classmates always

le school — junior
worst. Even after
emember the hor-
to her — not only
ce. She could still
to play on her.
rent.
ome and lock her-
r eyes out.

As a little girl, she'd always been chubby. Her grandmother said she just had baby fat and said that she'd eventually outgrow it. But when she started junior high, the baby fat was still there. It seemed like all her other female classmates were tall and thin, like models, and she still looked like a blob. The girls started dressing differently, too, wearing tiny skirts, high heels, and cute tops, but Natalie wasn't able to transform herself the way that they had. As a result, she looked even more different and everyone noticed, especially the guys, who started calling the other girls for dates.

No one called her.

But they did start calling her names.

She couldn't remember when it started, but suddenly, they were calling her Fatalie. Miss Big Bones. Flabtastica.

One time they called the local pizzeria and had four pizzas delivered to her house. Minutes later, someone called and asked if she had enjoyed the "snack" they had sent over. Another time they sent her a year-long membership to the Pie of the Month Club. They mailed her gift certificates for all-you-can-eat buffets, as well as coupons for Slim-Fast and Lean Cuisine.

She had never done anything to any of them, but for some reason, they decided that she deserved to be laughed at and made fun of. The one thing she *never* did was let them know how much their mean words and jokes hurt. She wouldn't give them the satisfaction. And it wasn't like she didn't have any friends. She did, but the girls she hung out with were also considered outcasts. So if Natalie wasn't being teased because of her weight, she was being teased along with her friends. There was never any escape.

Until the end of eighth grade.

That was when Natalie's parents told her they were moving to another town.

"I think you're overreacting," Eden said, cutting into Natalie's thoughts.

Claudia shook her head. "Trust me, she was lying. And I'm going to expose her."

"How?" Natalie asked as she tossed her long blonde hair over one shoulder.

"On Saturday night. At my party. I'm sure she's going to come alone, with some sort of lame story as to why her so-called boyfriend couldn't make it. All it's going to take is a couple of questions from me to show everyone what a liar she is."

"Is that all you're eating for lunch?" Eden asked, pointing at Natalie's strawberry yogurt, granola bar, and cup of fresh fruit.

"I had a big breakfast," Natalie said, remembering the blueberry pancakes and bacon she'd had. Yum!

"I wish I had your willpower," Eden said, opening a packet of ketchup and squeezing it over her cheeseburger and french fries.

"I don't think you have to worry about the way you look," Natalie said, and it was true. Tall and willowy, with chocolate-brown skin and straight black hair that reached down her back, Eden was gorgeous. Natalie thought she was just as beautiful as some of the girls who competed on Eden's favorite TV show, *America's Next Top Model.* Okay, okay, so every so often a clunker model slipped in, but Eden really was a knockout and most of the guys at North Ridge High thought so.

They thought the same thing about Natalie, too.

And it all started the summer she moved to North Ridge.

That summer, Natalie decided to do something about her weight. She wasn't going to wait to "outgrow" her baby fat. If she wanted to lose those extra pounds, she needed to do something about it. So she started exercising, slowly at first, with long walks and bicycle rides. Then she progressed to jogging and swimming. After that, she joined a gym and began working with a physical trainer.

When it came to food, she still ate what she wanted. She just monitored her portions and cut out a lot of junk food. Gone were the potato chips, candy bars, and ice-cream cones that she used to eat without thinking. When her mother baked, did she really need to eat four chocolate chip cookies when two were enough?

At the same time, she *finally* went through a major growth spurt and added four inches to her height.

As a result of everything, the pounds melted away, and by September she didn't recognize the willowy, blonde, blue-eyed girl in her bedroom mirror. Finally, she was able to wear the same cute clothes and high heels as her ex-classmates. When classes started in September, the old Natalie was gone, replaced by a new one.

It was like she was being given a clean slate.

Even though she was now thin, Natalie still

exercised and watched what she ate. Sure, there were some days when she didn't go jogging or she skipped the gym. And there were days when she felt like being a couch potato and plopped herself in front of the TV with a bag of Cool Ranch Doritos or barbecue-flavored Lay's. When too many of those days happened, all Natalie had to do was remember the way she used to be teased or look at old photos in her family photo album. It was usually the wake-up call she needed to get back on track.

After three years, Natalie still couldn't believe she was thin and pretty. And that guys were interested in her!

When it came to guys, she was pretty much shy around them and hadn't dated much. For the last month, she had been going out with Tom Marland, but only because he was Chase's best friend and Claudia had constantly been pressuring her to go out with him. To get Claudia off her back, she finally agreed to go to a movie with Tom. It hadn't been *too* hard to say yes to him when he'd called to ask her out. Tom was tall and buff, with white-blond hair and sea-green eyes — he looked exactly like a California beach boy. One date led to another and another and now it seemed like they were a couple. But it didn't feel that way to Natalie. Tom was definitely a catch, but she didn't feel like she *really* knew him. Or that he knew her. Whenever they went out on dates, it was always in a group, usually with Claudia and Chase and the rest of their clique. They never had any "alone" time and that's what she felt was missing. When you were "into" someone, didn't you want to spend time *just* with them? Natalie *never* got that sense from Tom, and she never saw him looking at her the way she saw other guys looking at their girlfriends. Those guys looked at their girlfriends with complete and total adoration.

She hated to admit it, but sometimes she felt the only reason Tom kept going out with her was because he thought she was hot. He liked the way she looked and he liked the other guys at North Ridge High to see that she was dating him. But she didn't want to be some guy's piece of arm candy!

Having never been in love before, Natalie wasn't sure what she should be feeling. How did you know when a guy you're going out with was *the one*?

Claudia speared a tomato with her fork and popped it into her mouth. "You and Tom are coming to my party, right?" Claudia asked Natalie.

Natalie shrugged. "I guess. Unless he has plans to go skiing."

"Scrap the skiing!" Claudia exclaimed. "You're coming to my party and you're bringing your boyfriend. Natalie, you can't let Tom walk all over you. You have to start calling the shots!"

Natalie knew there was no arguing with Claudia. When she told you to do something, you did it. But Tom was the same way. They were always doing what *he* wanted to do. He never asked her opinion or consulted with her when it came to their dates. He called all the shots and Natalie was starting to resent it. Didn't her opinion matter?

"Jennifer is *so* going to regret coming to my party," Claudia said.

It was on the tip of Natalie's tongue to ask Claudia if she liked being so mean. But she didn't. She didn't want Claudia to turn that anger on her. Over the last couple of months, it seemed that Claudia was becoming meaner and meaner. Most of the girls at North Ridge High were afraid of Claudia. They didn't want to cross her or get on her bad side. On more than one occasion, Claudia had been known to rip a girl to shreds with a catty comment or two. She was also notorious for getting people uninvited to parties and spreading untrue gossip. You never knew what Claudia was going to do.

A part of Natalie wanted to warn Jennifer not to come to Claudia's party, but she couldn't. If she did, Claudia would try to find out why Jennifer didn't show up. And if she *did* find out, Claudia would forget all about her feud with Jennifer and Natalie would be next on her hit list.

She couldn't take that chance.

She could only hope that Jennifer had been telling the truth and that she hadn't lied to Claudia.

"What have I done?" Jennifer moaned, ignoring her lunch and wanting to smack her head on the cafeteria table. Maybe that would knock some sense into her. "What have I done?"

"You lied," Violet said, beginning to count off on her fingers. "You told Claudia you had a boyfriend. You told her you and your boyfriend were going to be voted Most Romantic. And you told her you'd be going to her party on Saturday night. With your boyfriend!"

"It was a rhetorical question!" Jennifer exclaimed. "You don't have to remind me of my mistakes."

"If I don't, who will?" Violet pushed away her own untouched lunch tray. "What are you going to do?"

Jennifer shrugged as she reached into her backpack for a pad of paper and a pen. "What else can I do? I really don't have any other options."

"Phew! I'm *so* glad you're going to confess. I'm sure Claudia will make your life a living hell at first but eventually it will be over and she'll move on to torturing someone else."

"Confess?" Jennifer stared at Violet like she was crazy. "Who said anything about confessing?"

"Huh?"

"I need to start working on my essay," Jennifer said as she began writing on the pad. "That'll be the easy part. Once my essay is done, then we can concentrate on finding a boyfriend."

Violet gulped. "You mean you're still going to go through with it?"

Jennifer glanced up from the pad. "Of course I am! You didn't really think I was going to confess to Claudia, did you?"

Violet squirmed in her seat. "Well . . ."

Jennifer's brown eyes widened with shock. "And give her the satisfaction of being right? Never!" She started writing again.

"We could ask one of my cousins to pretend to be your boyfriend," Violet suggested. "I'm sure Shermy would do it. He likes you."

Jennifer gave Violet a grateful smile as she looked up from her pad again and tossed her long red hair over one shoulder. "Thanks for the offer, but that isn't going to work."

"Why not?"

"Not only do I need a boyfriend, but I need a *hot* boyfriend."

"A hot boyfriend," Violet repeated.

Jennifer nodded. "He's got to be a guy who's going to make Claudia super jealous. I want her to wish that he was going out with her."

"*Why* do you always have to make things super complicated?" Violet moaned. "Why? Why?

Why? First we needed to find you a boyfriend. Now we need to find you a *hot* boyfriend. What next? He owns a Mercedes and his father is a millionaire?"

"That would be great, but let's get realistic," Jennifer said as she kept writing on her pad.

"You're the one who needs the reality check, Jen!" Violet snapped, losing her patience with her best friend. "With Valentine's Day only a week away, every girl at North Ridge High who has a boyfriend is going to be clinging to him."

Jennifer shrugged. "And that's a problem? Relax, Vi. You're stressing out for no reason. It's all going to work out. Trust me."

"I do trust you," Violet said, pushing her sliding glasses back up her nose. "Sorry I lost my temper. I guess I'm just worried, that's all."

"Well, stop worrying," Jennifer insisted. "There are plenty of other hotties at North Ridge High. All we have to do is find *one*."

"But which one?" Violet asked as they stared around the cafeteria.

If Eden heard Claudia say another word about Jennifer, she was going to scream!

All morning long Claudia had been going on

ennifer and her fake boy-
ly! If Jennifer was lying
nd, then she probably had
though, she wasn't con-
so-called problems. She
vn and they were real.
om her boyfriend, Keith,
n. Two days had gone by
him and that wasn't like
alling and text messaging

to connect with him since
hadn't returned any of her
f her texts. And she hadn't
ol.
e was avoiding her.

v what.
finding out.
s scanned the cafeteria,
wouldn't be hard to miss.
l and super muscular, with
d and a tiny diamond ear-

feeling in the pit of her
ling she usually got when

she sensed a guy was getting ready to break up with her. But why would Keith want to break up with her? They had just started dating a month ago, and the way they had hooked up was *so* sweet. Like something out of a movie! She was on the cheerleading squad and she'd caught his eye right before a basketball home game had started. When he came over to say hi, they started chatting, and when it was time for the game to begin, she told him that if he got six baskets, she'd go out with him. That night he got twelve. At the end of the game, after North Ridge High had won, he came over to Eden and told her that she owed him two dates. *And* a kiss. Eden happily agreed and asked him when he wanted his kiss. He collected the kiss that night in his car when he drove her home.

What could be wrong? She thought everything was great between them. True, it sometimes seemed like they didn't have a lot in common, but opposites attracted, right?

Eden chewed on her lower lip. She hated to admit it, but Claudia might know something. After all, Chase and Keith were both on the basketball team and they were friends. Maybe

ıing to Chase and Chase
› Claudia. But if he had,
entioned it? Was she try-
s?
say anything to Claudia,
:oss the crowded cafete-
ight of him and the heavy
stomach disappeared.
gh, it returned when she
with long braids come by
ırm around his waist.
:ve what she was seeing.
ıd, and another girl had
e he was *hers*. That was
gh Eden wanted to run
ınd shove that girl away
t. Instead, she found her
sent Keith a text message,
er house after school. She
into the pocket of his let-
ılled out his cell phone,

:t horrified Eden.
ıer back, Keith closed his
ıis pocket, and walked out
:he girl. Not only was her

arm still wrapped around his waist, but Keith had an arm wrapped around her shoulders. The girl smiled up at Keith and snuggled up against him as they walked away.

Staring at the two of them, Eden blinked back tears. She hated to admit it, but it looked like her boyfriend had found himself a new girlfriend.

Chapter Three

"So do you think my party should have a theme?" Claudia asked Natalie as they walked home after school. "I'm thinking since next week is Valentine's Day, I should play that up. Lots of pink and red decorations. Lots of chocolate desserts. Maybe even a chocolate fountain! Wouldn't that be yummy?"

Natalie nodded. She knew her opinion really didn't matter. Claudia always did what she wanted to do.

"Maybe I should make everyone dress in red, and if they're not in red, I won't let them in."

"Do you really want to play fashion police the entire night?"

Claudia thought about it for a second. "Good point. Maybe I'll tell all the girls that *I'm* the only one allowed to dress in red for the party."

Natalie knew if Claudia did that none of the girls would dare disobey. Crossing Claudia was like being sent to Siberia. You would be frozen out of all social events once she got the word out to her friends.

For the second time that day, Natalie wondered why Claudia enjoyed being so mean. Was it a power thing? Did she feel she *had* to be this way? Was she afraid that if everyone wasn't scared of her, they wouldn't be her friend? Although, realistically, were the other girls Claudia hung out with her friends?

Natalie liked to think that she and Claudia were friends. She listened when Claudia had problems and tried to help her out when she could. They certainly spent a lot of time together. During the summer they went to the beach and Claudia's parents' country club. They went shopping together in Manhattan, saw Broadway matinees, went to concerts, had sleepovers, hung out at the mall, borrowed each other's clothes, and discussed guys. In the beginning, Natalie had loved hanging out with Claudia. She'd been fun! But lately . . . lately Natalie just wasn't *liking* Claudia.

She knew she couldn't say anything to her. No one dared to criticize Claudia. But maybe she

Unit #9
Glenn Raymond School

could discuss the situation with Eden and see what she thought.

Natalie felt closer to Eden than she did to Claudia. Eden was more real and grounded. True, she was a girly girl, *totally* into shopping and hair and makeup and guys, but Natalie felt that if she were ever in a crisis, she could depend on Eden. Eden was the one who always brought over her homework when she was out sick. Eden was the one who had come with her to the hospital last month to visit her grandmother after she broke her leg and helped her parents plan her Sweet Sixteen surprise party last summer. She couldn't keep track of all the nice things Eden had done for her since freshman year. If she ever had a problem and needed to talk it out, all she had to do was pick up the phone or send a text and Eden was there.

Thinking about Eden made Natalie realize that she had to call her later. At lunch, she could see that something was bothering her. At one point it looked like she was crying, but Eden had reassured her that she wasn't. Something had gotten into her eye, she quickly explained. Before Natalie could ask her anything else, Eden had dashed off to the bathroom. Natalie hadn't seen her the rest of the day and she hadn't been waiting with Claudia after school. She hoped she was okay.

As Natalie and Claudia walked toward Natalie's house, a young woman in her late twenties came running out of the house next door. It was a Victorian three-story that was identical to Natalie's house, although her neighbors still had their Christmas decorations up. Bright-colored lights were strung across the front porch and Santa and his sleigh were still positioned on the front lawn. At the sight of Natalie, the woman waved and hurried over.

"Natalie!" she exclaimed. "You don't know how glad I am to see you!"

Natalie smiled at the petite brunette. "Hi, Lisa! What's up?"

Lisa Barnes was Natalie's next-door neighbor. She and her husband, Stan, and their four-year-old daughter, Bonnie, had moved in last fall. Natalie had babysat for Bonnie twice.

"My babysitter canceled on me and I was wondering if I could ask a favor. I have to take my mom to a doctor's appointment and I really don't want to take Bonnie with me. With it being flu season, the last thing I want to do is expose her to a waiting room full of germs. Could you watch her for me? I shouldn't be very long. An hour, two tops."

"Sure!" Natalie didn't even have to think about it. She loved kids and hoped to become a nursery school teacher after college. One reason why she loved little kids so much was that they didn't judge you. They saw what was on the inside, rather than what was on the outside.

"You're a lifesaver!" Lisa squealed, giving Natalie a hug and racing back inside.

"I thought we were going to talk about my party." Claudia pouted as Natalie followed after Lisa.

"We can still do that."

Claudia wrinkled her nose, like she had smelled something bad. "I don't do little kids."

"Bonnie's a sweetie."

"She isn't one of those rug rats that has a runny nose and grubby hands?" Claudia skeptically asked.

"You're going to love her. Trust me. She's an angel!"

Bonnie had turned into a devil.

When Natalie first walked in the door,

Bonnie came running over. She was an adorable little girl with two pigtails and a scattering of freckles across her cheeks, wearing pink overalls and a pink turtleneck. Before Natalie even had a chance to take off her coat, Bonnie had given her a hug. Natalie had hugged her back, inhaling the scent of Johnson & Johnson's baby shampoo, peanut butter, and Magic Markers. Then Bonnie had wanted to give Claudia a hug. Natalie couldn't help but giggle as Claudia knelt down and allowed Bonnie to wrap her arms around her.

"So soft!" Bonnie had squealed while pressing her face against Claudia's cashmere sweater.

"And expensive," Claudia had said while awkwardly trying to pull away from Bonnie, who had her in a death grip.

"You're pretty," Bonnie had said, giving Claudia a big wet kiss.

"She's gotten a little clingy lately," Lisa whispered into Natalie's ear as she sneaked into the kitchen to use the back door. "She hates when I go anywhere without her. She might give you a little bit of a hard time, but she'll get over it. Hopefully this phase isn't going to last much longer."

"Don't worry about it," Natalie had reassured Lisa as she watched her walk out. "Bonnie and I are old friends. I'm sure we're going to get along fine."

At first they had. Bonnie had taken Natalie and Claudia into her playroom and shown them her dolls. Instead of giving them names, Bonnie gave each doll a number. "This is Seven, this is Eleven, this is Forty-Four," Bonnie explained. Then she dropped the rag doll she was holding and her eyes widened with fear. It was like she had suddenly realized something. First she looked at Natalie. Then she turned to look at Claudia. After that, she looked around the playroom, frantically searching for the person she now knew was missing. "M-M-Mommy?"

"Mommy had to go run an errand," Natalie said. "She'll be back soon."

As soon as Natalie said those words, Bonnie's lower lip started to tremble. "No Mommy?" She ran out of the playroom, screaming at the top of her lungs. "MOMMMMEEEEEE!!!!!"

"That was the right thing to say," Claudia stated sarcastically.

"How was I supposed to know she would freak out?"

Natalie hurried out of the playroom and found Bonnie struggling to open the front door.

"Don't cry, Bonnie," she begged, wrapping her arms around her and moving her away from the door. "Mommy will be back soon."

"MOMMMEEEEEEEEE!!!" Bonnie wailed, tears streaming down her face. "I WANT MY MOMMEEE!!!!"

Bonnie broke free of Natalie's hold and began jumping up and down, stomping on the floor, screaming at the top of her lungs. She was having a full-force temper tantrum.

Claudia pressed her hand over her ears. "Sorry, Nat, but I told you I don't do rug rats. That screaming is driving me crazy. I'm gone!"

And with those final words, Claudia grabbed her coat and hurried out the front door, leaving Natalie all alone.

Eden's eyes were red and swollen.

She had been crying in her bedroom for the last half hour after getting a text message from Keith telling her that he was breaking up with her.

A text message!

He didn't even have the guts to break up with her in person. How cold could a guy get?

After her last class, Eden had waited by Keith's locker but he never showed up. She wanted to talk to him about what was going on between them. Correction. She wanted to talk about what was *not* going on between them. And who was the girl she had seen him with at lunch? He owed her at least that much, didn't he?

After waiting forty-five minutes for Keith, Eden finally gave up and came home. But the entire time, she had been wondering where he was and it had driven her crazy. Because all she could think about was *that* girl. What did she have that Eden didn't? What made her so special that Keith wanted to be with her instead?

Seconds after she walked through the front door, she had gotten Keith's text.

She still didn't understand *why* he was breaking up with her.

All his text message had said was: IT'S OVER.

Eden reached across her bed for another tissue to blow her nose. As she did, the doorbell rang. Eden's heart began pounding. Could it be

Keith? Was he having second thoughts? Maybe he was coming over to apologize and ask her to take him back. If that were true, what would she do?

If Chase had done this to Claudia, she knew exactly what Claudia would do. She would make Chase grovel before taking him back.

But she wasn't Claudia and she didn't like playing games.

If Keith wanted her to take him back, she would!

Eden raced down the front staircase and flung open the front door. When she saw who was standing on the porch, the smile on her face disappeared.

It was Claudia.

The last person she wanted to see.

What was she doing here? She was supposed to be spending the afternoon with Natalie. Now she was going to have to tell her what had happened.

Claudia instantly noticed her blotchy face and tears.

"What's wrong?" she asked as she walked inside. "Why are you crying?"

"Keith broke up with me," she sniffed.

Back in her bedroom, Eden told Claudia the entire story. When she was finished, Claudia had a stern look on her face.

"You can't let him get away with this!"

Eden knew that Claudia was all about getting even and settling the score, making sure no one took advantage of her. But that wasn't Eden. It took too much time and energy to hold a grudge. She tried to treat people the way she wanted to be treated. If they didn't, she moved on.

She wished Natalie were sitting across from her. Natalie would know what to say to make her feel better. And she'd give her advice about what to do.

Eden crumpled the tissue in her hand, tossing it into the wastebasket by her desk. "It's over. Done with. Time to move on."

"But don't you want to know why he's breaking up with you?"

Eden waved her cell phone in Claudia's face. "Ever since I got his text message, I've been calling him. I've sent my own texts. He won't answer."

Claudia rolled her eyes. "That's so typical of a guy."

"What am I supposed to do if he won't talk to me?"

"You *make* him talk to you," Claudia insisted.

"How?"

"You confront him. If he wants to break up with you, he has to do it in person."

Eden looked at Claudia like she was crazy. "Get dumped twice? I don't think so! Once was painful enough."

"Then at least give him a piece of your mind. Don't let him off the hook so easily. You think I didn't see him in the cafeteria today with his new girlfriend? I did!"

"Why didn't you say anything?"

"I didn't want you to feel bad."

Eden was stunned. This was so unlike Claudia!

"After all, what is this? The fourth guy who's dumped you in the last six months?" Claudia didn't wait for an answer. "Not that I'm keeping track. Maybe you should get some relationship books from the library. It could help you avoid making the same mistakes. Obviously, you're doing something wrong with every guy you go out with."

Eden couldn't believe what she was hearing!

She had thought Claudia was trying to make her feel better. Instead, she was being critical! The way she always was!

"Pay attention to Chase and me," Claudia said before Eden could say anything. "We're the perfect couple. That's why we're going to be voted Most Romantic at the Valentine's Day dance next week."

Eden hated to admit it, but Claudia and Chase *were* the perfect couple. They'd been together forever. What was their secret, and what was she doing wrong? Why did the guys she went out with keep dumping her? She was a pretty girl and guys were always asking her out on dates. She'd gone out with four different guys since September. Why didn't anything last beyond a month? Was she unlovable? Was that what it was?

Eden could feel tears welling in her eyes again. She reached for another tissue and blew her nose.

She didn't know what to do.

All she did know was that she was going to be alone on Valentine's Day.

That thought made her cry even more.

★ ★ ★

"Bonnie, please stop crying. *Please*," Natalie begged. "If you stop crying, I'll buy you any toy you want."

Natalie hated resorting to blackmail, but what else could she do? Claudia had been gone for twenty minutes and Bonnie was *still* crying and showing no signs of winding down. Where did she find the energy?

Natalie had tried everything to get Bonnie to stop crying. She sang, she danced. She offered to put on her favorite DVDs, play with her toys, bake cookies. Nothing worked. Bonnie just kept crying and crying, running from room to room and screaming at the top of her lungs. She was like one of those car alarms that wouldn't turn off!

What if someone walking by heard Bonnie crying? She didn't want them to think she was hurting her. And whoever said toddlers went through the Terrible Twos had never dealt with Bonnie and the Terrible Fours!

Natalie wished she wasn't all alone. How could Claudia have left her? Duh! Dumb question. Because that was Claudia. The only person she ever thought about was herself. Eden never would have left her alone. Eden would have stayed and tried to help calm Bonnie down. Instead, she was all alone with no clue about what to do! This was crazy! She couldn't let a four-year-old defeat her!

Then Natalie heard it. The sound of the doorbell.

Natalie raced to answer it. Anything to get away from Bonnie and her tears.

She opened the front door and as she did, the crying stopped.

"Uncle Leo!" Bonnie happily shrieked, running across the front hall and throwing her arms around the legs of the teenage guy standing on the porch.

Natalie recognized Leo Barnes. Everyone at North Ridge High knew who Leo was. Overweight Leo was known for his huge appetite and huge size. He wasn't flabby fat — he didn't jiggle when he walked — but he *was* fat and could stand to lose some weight. He definitely had a big belly, although he didn't have a double chin. He had a mop of crazy brown curls on his head and gold-flecked green eyes.

Leo would eat anything if someone dared him to. Last semester someone had offered him twenty dollars to eat a whole can of sardines. He had.

Natalie often wondered what Leo went through. Even though Leo had a bunch of friends at North Ridge High, a lot of students laughed at him behind his back. They called him the Human Garbage Disposal and Mr. Jelly Belly. They asked if he had his own zip code or if he needed to buy two seats when he was on a plane.

If the barbs bothered him, Leo never let it show. He always had a smile on his face and was ready to help someone out if they needed his assistance. Every Christmas he volunteered as Santa Claus in the children's wing of the local hospital.

Natalie never laughed at Leo or made fun of him. Her heart went out to him because she knew exactly what he was going through.

"Hey, peanut! What's up? What's with the tears? Big girls don't cry. Is Natalie not being nice to you?"

"How do you know my name?" Natalie asked in surprise.

Leo rolled his eyes. "Everyone knows your name. You're one of the popular girls from school. Unlike me, who's unpopular."

"What's unpopular?" Bonnie asked, wiping her runny nose across her sleeve.

Leo lifted Bonnie into his arms and gave her a kiss on the cheek before putting her back down. "Something you'll never be!"

"I didn't know you were Bonnie's uncle."

Leo squeezed Bonnie's nose with two fingers and hid it behind his back. "Oh no! I stole your nose!"

Bonnie giggled as she touched the tip of her nose. "No, you didn't, Uncle Leo. It's still here."

"Are you sure?"

Leo turned to Natalie. "My brother Stan is married to Lisa. She gave me a call on my cell phone a little while ago. She was worried you might be having some problems with Bonnie," he said, putting his fingers back on Bonnie's nose before pressing his mouth to her belly and making a farting sound. Bonnie instantly erupted into a burst of giggles. "I can see she was right. Someone was being bad!" he scolded. "Tell Natalie you're sorry for crying when Mommy went away."

Bonnie stared down at the floor, twisting her right foot into the carpet. Then she stared at Natalie from beneath her bangs. "Sorry," she whispered.

"Good girl," Leo said, kissing her on top of her head.

"I wouldn't say you're unpopular," Natalie told Leo. She didn't know why, but Leo calling himself unpopular bothered her. It made her feel like he thought she was better than him, and that wasn't true.

Bonnie began tugging Leo by the hand, trying to drag him into the living room. "Uncle Leo, come and have a tea party with me!"

"A tea party! Really?" Leo happily clapped his hands. "Oh boy!"

Natalie watched as Bonnie led Leo to a tiny table and chairs situated in the corner of the living room. Leo couldn't fit into the chair, but he got down on his knees and let Bonnie drape a purple feather boa around his neck and place a huge straw hat on his head. Bonnie then added a colorful silk scarf to her own neck and sat across from Leo. She reached for a pink teapot and poured her uncle a cup.

"This tea is deee-liss-eee-us!" Leo proclaimed with a loud slurp. He held out his cup. "More, please!"

Natalie couldn't help but laugh at the sight of Leo sitting at Bonnie's table. They looked so cute together. It was obvious that he adored his niece and she adored him.

"Hey, Natalie, want to join our tea party?" Leo looked at Bonnie. "It's okay if Natalie joins us, isn't it?"

Bonnie's head bobbed up and down. "Yes!"

"I'd love to," Natalie said, hurrying to join them.

Chapter Four

"How's your essay coming?" Violet asked, looking up from her American History notes.

"What essay?" Jennifer asked as she ripped a piece of lined yellow paper from her notepad, crumpled it, and tossed it on the floor, where it joined a growing pile in the corner of her kitchen. Her Siamese cat, Sheba, walked over and sniffed the page. After discovering it wasn't something edible, she twitched her tail and walked out of the kitchen.

"I thought you said writing the essay was going to be the easy part."

"So did I." Jennifer sighed. She had been trying to write her essay for the last three hours, ever since she and Violet had come to her house after classes had ended. She still didn't have anything on paper. "I was wrong. How can I write about my perfect boyfriend and our perfect relationship when I don't know anything about him?"

"You don't have to know anything about him," Violet pointed out. "Just make it all up! The deadline for essays is Friday. You have to write one. Otherwise, you can't compete."

"I'm trying, but the words aren't coming out. Whatever I say needs to fit the guy I wind up with. And because I don't know anything about him, I'm having a hard time."

"Can't you give him a copy of your essay once you find him? You're going to have to do that anyway so your stories are straight."

"Yes, but it's not the same thing. If I knew something, *anything*, about him, it might make the writing easier."

"Why don't you write about the guy you wish was already your boyfriend?" Violet suggested.

"There isn't anyone at school," Jennifer said.

Violet shook her head. "That's not what I meant. Don't you sometimes wonder who you're going to marry someday? What he looks like, how you fall in love with him, how he proposes to you?"

"Not really. Why? Do you?"

Violet slowly nodded her head. "I'm going to meet him in college during our sophomore year and I'm going to be late for class. We're going to crash into each other in the hallway and our books are going to fall to the floor. He's going to help me pick everything up, but before I can thank him, he's running off to his class. One thing I notice about him is how messy he is. His clothes are all wrinkly and look too big on him and he needs a haircut. The other thing I notice are his eyes. They're big and brown and there's something about them that I can't forget."

Violet left her seat at the butcher-block table and walked over to the stainless-steel refrigerator, reaching in for a bottle of water. She opened it up and took a sip. "Later that day I run into him at the campus coffee shop and I offer to buy him a coffee. We talk for hours and he walks me back to my dorm. After he does, he asks if I'm doing anything on Saturday night. At first I want to play hard to get and pretend I already have plans, but I like him so much that I say yes. On our first date, he takes me bowling and then we go out for Chinese food and he teaches me how to use chopsticks. When he takes me home and kisses me good night, I know that he's the guy I'm going to marry. And when he does propose to me during our senior year, it's going to be at the same Chinese restaurant where we had our first date. When I crack open my fortune cookie at the end of dinner, my fortune is going to say, *Will you marry me?* Of course my answer will be yes!"

"Violet Wagner!" Jennifer exclaimed. "Who knew you were such a romantic!"

Violet blushed as she sat back down next to Jennifer. "You don't daydream like that?"

Jennifer reached for Violet's bottle of water and took a sip. "I'm too busy worrying if I'm going to have a date for the prom. I have plenty of time to worry about finding a groom."

"Do you want me to write the essay for you?" Violet offered.

Jennifer shook her head. "Thanks, but I have to do this myself. Don't worry, it'll get done."

"You're still going to have to find the guy you're writing about," Violet gently reminded. "Saturday night isn't that far away."

"I know," Jennifer groaned. "I know."

"You probably don't want to hear this, but there's still time to back out."

Jennifer stubbornly shook her head. "And give Claudia the satisfaction of knowing I lied? I don't think so!"

"But if you don't confess now and you still don't have a boyfriend by Saturday night, what are you going to do?"

Jennifer didn't say anything. She just stared at Violet, who gasped.

"You're not going to go to her party *alone*, are you?"

"Why not?"

"Because you'll be humiliated."

"I'm not going to hide!" Jennifer exclaimed. "That's what she expects me to do. She thinks I won't show up, but I will. I'm not afraid of Claudia. Besides, once I go to her party, it'll be over and done with. Like ripping off a Band-Aid."

"Ouch!"

"I still have tomorrow and Friday to find someone. Don't count me out yet." Jennifer pushed her chair away from the table. "I don't know about you, but I'm hungry. How about we order a pizza? My parents are both working late tonight so it would be nice not to eat alone. Maybe after I have something to eat, I'll be able to write my essay."

"Sure. Let me just call my mom and tell her

I'm not going to be home for dinner," Violet said, whipping out her cell.

Jennifer walked over to the counter and opened the drawer where there were a bunch of take-out menus. Jennifer's mother, who worked long hours at an advertising agency, didn't cook much and was always ordering in. Jennifer started searching for the pizzeria menus so she could find a place to call. "How does half pepperoni, half mushroom sound?"

"Sounds yummy!" Violet exclaimed as her stomach rumbled in agreement.

Thirty minutes later, there was a knock on the back door.

"Pizza!" Violet happily exclaimed, closing her textbooks.

Jennifer rummaged for her wallet in her shoulder bag before going to open the door. As she walked across the kitchen, Violet called out, "Wouldn't it be great if we could order up a boyfriend the way we just ordered this pizza?"

Jennifer laughed. "If only!"

Then Jennifer opened the back door and was left speechless when she saw the delivery guy.

He was *gorgeous.*

His face was all chiseled cheekbones, with a small cleft in his chin. His jet-black hair was straight and parted on the side, falling smoothly across his forehead and bringing attention to his piercing blue eyes. He was wearing a green plaid flannel shirt with a white waffle T-shirt underneath it and a black leather vest on top. His jeans were faded and his motorcycle boots were dusty and scuffed.

Jennifer instantly knew who he was.

Every girl at North Ridge High did.

Will Sinclair.

The Heartbreaker.

He held out the pizza box. "Are you Jennifer Harris? Half pepperoni, half mushroom?"

"Come in," Jennifer said, holding the back door wide open. "You must be freezing out there."

The scent of hot pizza brought Sheba running into the kitchen. Immediately, she began rubbing herself up against Will's leg and purring.

"Would you excuse us for a second?" Jennifer asked Will, grabbing Violet by the arm and dragging her into the next room. "I can't seem to find my wallet and I need help finding it."

"Isn't that it in your hand?" Will pointed out.

Jennifer stared at the red leather wallet she was holding and laughed. "It is! But there's no money in it. I need to go find my other wallet. We'll be right back."

As soon as they were alone, Jennifer whispered, "Are you thinking what I'm thinking?"

"You want Will Sinclair to be your boyfriend."

"He's perfect!"

"Perfectly awful!" Behind her glasses, Violet's blue eyes widened with concern. "Jen, you've heard the stories about him."

Jennifer knew what Violet was talking about. Will was a notorious serial dater. He never went out with the same girl more than twice and his dates weren't just limited to girls from North Ridge High. He was known to have gone out with girls from St. Bernadette's and St. Edmund's, two all-girls Catholic high schools, as well as two other public high schools. It was even rumored that he'd gone out with girls in college sororities!

Girls at North Ridge High were always following him down the halls. Waiting by his locker before and after school. Sitting at his table in the school cafeteria. They offered to buy his lunch.

Do his homework. Take him to concerts and movies. Tempt him with expensive gifts.

But Will never said yes to them.

He dated only the girls that he wanted to date and then moved on. It didn't matter if a girl was still interested in going out with him. Saying yes to a date with Will Sinclair meant maybe having your heart broken. Because there was always the chance that he might not call back. That was why he was called the Heartbreaker.

But girls kept saying yes to him because each and every one of them thought that *she* was going to be the one to get Will to change his ways. He was a bad boy, and there was nothing more irresistible to a good girl than trying to tame a bad boy.

Jennifer felt that Will would be *perfect* as her fake boyfriend. If everyone thought she had tamed the Heartbreaker, she'd be the talk of North Ridge High.

"Those stories are nothing but gossip," Jennifer said dismissively. "You shouldn't be so quick to judge him!"

"I'm not judging him. All I know is what I've heard."

"Well, you've heard wrong!"

"Are you sure this is such a good idea?" Violet worriedly asked. "Are people really going to buy you and Will as a couple?"

"I think you just insulted me!" Jennifer gasped in mock outrage.

"He's never had a girlfriend," Violet reminded her. "Don't take it personally. People are going to talk. Why all of a sudden does he decide to have a girlfriend?"

"What can I say? He was waiting for the right girl. Me!"

"I don't know, Jennifer. Something could go wrong."

"Nothing is going to go wrong. How can it? And think of the best part! When I walk into Claudia's party on Saturday night, her eyes are going to pop right out of her head. I need her to be shocked when she sees Will on my arm. Can you think of a better secret boyfriend than him?"

Before Violet could answer, Will called out from the kitchen. "Hey! Your pizza is getting cold!"

"I'm going to ask him!" Jennifer announced, hurrying back into the kitchen.

Will had put the pizza box on top of the

table. Sheba had already jumped onto a chair and was pressing her nose to the box, whiskers twitching. Jennifer shooed her away and she jumped back down on the floor, meowing.

"That's fifteen dollars," Will said.

"Fifteen dollars," Jennifer repeated, opening up her wallet.

"I thought you said you didn't have any money in that wallet," Will pointed out.

Jennifer laughed as she scrambled to say something that made sense. "My wallets are identical. I liked this one so much, I had to have two of them. It's a girl thing."

"Whatever."

Jennifer handed Will the money for the pizza, along with a generous tip. Will counted the bills and then folded them, putting them in his back pocket. He gave Jennifer a smile for the tip. "Thanks! Enjoy the pizza."

Violet nudged Jennifer. "He's leaving! If you're going to ask him, ask him!"

"So listen!" Jennifer called out. "I know you're going to think this sounds crazy, but I need you to be my boyfriend."

Will turned around and stared at Jennifer, his blue eyes wide with disbelief. "Excuse me?"

"I've gotten myself into this . . . situation," Jennifer explained, trying not to squirm. "I told someone that I have a boyfriend. Which obviously I don't otherwise I wouldn't be standing here asking you to be my boyfriend."

"And why are you asking me? Why not some other guy?"

"Because you'd be perfect," Jennifer admitted. "Every girl at North Ridge High would love to go out with you."

Will folded his arms across his chest and Jennifer couldn't help but notice how muscular they were, even underneath all that flannel. "Have you ever wanted to go out with me?" he asked.

"I never really thought about it."

"So why now?"

Jennifer sighed. "Because I have to find someone by Friday."

"Why Friday?"

"That's the deadline for essays for the Most Romantic couple contest," Violet piped in.

Will held up a hand. "Wait a minute. Slow down. Not only do you want me to pretend to be your boyfriend, but you want us to compete as Most Romantic?"

"Yes," Jennifer admitted.

"It sounds like you've gotten yourself into a mess," Will said. "You should be careful about what you say."

"She speaks without thinking," Violet told Will. "It's a bad habit."

Will turned to Jennifer. "You should work on that."

"I will. In the future. I promise. But right now I need your help." She bit down on her lower lip, praying that Will would take pity on her. "Will you help me?"

"I don't even know you!" Will exclaimed.

"We can get to know each other," Jennifer suggested. "It's only for a week. Until Valentine's Day. After that, you're free!"

Will sighed and ran a hand through his hair. The smooth black strands fell back into place. "Look, you seem nice, but I don't like lying to people. It's not my style."

"Is that the only reason?" Jennifer asked.

"What do you mean?"

"Maybe there's another reason. Maybe you don't want people thinking you're off the market."

Will shrugged. "Well, there is that, too. I like

keeping myself in circulation. Sorry, I wish I could help you out, but I don't do girlfriends, real or fake."

Will turned around and headed for the back door.

Violet sighed. "Looks like Claudia wins again."

At the mention of Claudia's name, Will stopped in his tracks. "Claudia?" he asked, turning to face Jennifer and Violet. "Are you talking about Claudia Monroe?"

Jennifer nodded. "Yes. Why? Do you know her?"

Will made a face. "Do I ever! Not only has she stiffed me on tips in the past, but last month she had a huge party and ordered a bunch of pizzas. When I delivered them, she wound up not paying. The cost of the pizzas had to come out of my pocket. Why didn't you mention her name sooner? This changes everything."

"What do you mean?" Jennifer asked.

"If you're planning to pull a fast one on Claudia, then count me in."

Jennifer couldn't believe what she was hearing. "Does that mean you'll help me? You'll do it? You'll pretend to be my boyfriend?"

"Absolutely."

Before she could stop herself, Jennifer threw her arms around Will and gave him a hug. "Thank you! Thank you! Thank you! You don't know how much this means to me!"

As Jennifer hugged Will, she couldn't help but notice how nice he smelled. It was a combination of pizza, soap, and some sort of guy scent that was kind of woodsy.

Jennifer awkwardly broke the hug and stepped back. "Sorry about that. Sometimes I get a little overexcited."

Will rubbed his hands together and gave an evil Bart Simpson chuckle. "So, tell me what I have to do."

"One of our first tests is going to be a party that Claudia is throwing on Saturday night," Jennifer said. "Practically everyone at school is going to be there, waiting to see us, because Claudia thinks I'm not going to show with a boyfriend. I think we should spend as much time together as we can this week so we can get to know each other. Trust me, if we want to fool Claudia, then this is going to have to seem real."

Will nodded in agreement. "I hear you. Why don't you swing by the pizzeria tomorrow after school? We can hang out and work on our stories."

"It's a date!" Jennifer exclaimed.

"You mean a fake date," Will reminded her as he walked out the back door.

"Right!" Jennifer hurriedly agreed. "A fake date!"

Chapter Five

Thursday morning Eden was waiting in front of Keith's locker.

She was determined to talk to him. If he thought he could just send her a text message and that would be the end of things between them, he was wrong. All last night she had thought of what Claudia had told her and she was right. Keith owed her an explanation. She might not like what he told her, but she wanted to know why he was breaking up with her. And even though she hated to admit this, a teeny tiny part of her was hoping if they did talk, they might still have a chance to work things out. At the very least, Keith would get to hear what she had to say.

To make sure she didn't miss him, Eden had come to school an hour earlier than usual. She knew Keith was going to have to get his books for his morning classes, so he wouldn't be able to avoid her.

Eden stared down the mostly deserted hallway. It was weird not hearing a bunch of different conversations going on at the same time or the nonstop clanking of locker doors. It was so quiet! She had never come to school this early. Most of the students already here were the ones who were taking accelerated classes. They were already in the school library or computer center. Everyone she hung out with was still at home.

Thinking of the smart kids reminded Eden that she wasn't one of them. She did okay in her classes, but she wouldn't be taking any Advanced Placement classes next year the way her two older sisters had when they attended North Ridge High. Unlike Shannon and Alyssa, she wasn't a brainiac, and she wouldn't be winning a full college scholarship the way they both had. Shannon was a sophomore at NYU in the pre-med program, while Alyssa was a senior at Columbia and applying to law school.

Thinking of her sisters reminded Eden that she had a tutoring session that morning. Her parents, who were both lawyers, hadn't been thrilled with her PSAT scores last spring. With the SATs coming up in May, they had gotten her a tutor last month. Eden hadn't thought her scores were that bad — after all, it was a standardized test and you couldn't really study for it — but her parents disagreed. They felt that she wasn't applying herself enough, but that wasn't true! She just wasn't as smart as Shannon and Alyssa, and even though her parents didn't mean to do it, they were always comparing her to them. She knew they didn't do it on purpose, but they still did it when they said things like, "Shannon never had any trouble in Chemistry. Why don't you give her a call and see if she can help you out?" Or, "Alyssa already had enough credits from her Advanced Placement classes to enter Columbia as a sophomore. Why don't you think about taking a class or two this summer to finish your high school requirements and get a jump start?"

In a family of overachievers, Eden felt like she was an underachiever, even though she always tried to do her best. Her father was constantly telling her she needed to think about her future. Well, she did think about her future. She knew what she wanted to do when she was finished with college. She wanted to be a model.

She wanted to wear beautiful clothes, pose for photographers, and travel the world! She wanted to be the next Tyra Banks. Her favorite TV show was *America's Next Top Model* and she watched it religiously every week. Often, she would practice different facial expressions in her bedroom mirror and work on her runway walk. She also subscribed to all the fashion magazines like *Vogue, Elle, W,* and *Harper's Bazaar.* When it came to designers, stylists, models, and photographers, she knew everything, but she didn't share that information with her family. If they knew she wanted to be a model, she was sure they'd be horrified.

So she didn't tell them.

But someday she would.

Last night she had spent hours in front of her closet, going through her clothes, trying to find the perfect outfit for today. If Keith was going to break up with her, then she wanted him to see what he was losing.

In the end, she decided to wear a pink turtleneck with black jeans and gray and white fake-fur boots decorated with dangling pompoms on the side. She had decided not to put *too* much effort into it. No reason to let Keith know she was dressing for him! The look was very casual and "let's cuddle up in front of the fire at a ski lodge." She'd used a flat iron on her hair so it fell over her shoulders in a smooth sheet and dabbed only a tiny bit of smoky eye shadow and mascara on her lids and lashes so she could bring out the color of her chocolate-brown eyes.

After waiting for thirty minutes, Eden saw Keith walking down the hallway toward her. She fought against the butterflies in her stomach. She was so nervous! But she couldn't let him see that. She couldn't let him see that he had upset her — although her frantic messages and texts from yesterday proved the opposite. She had to be calm. If she wasn't calm, he wouldn't listen to her. Guys hated weepy, clingy girls.

As Keith got closer to his locker, he saw her. His gray eyes widened in surprise.

"What are you doing here so early?" he asked.

Eden closed the distance between them. Should she put her hand on his arm? She decided not to. It didn't feel right. There was something almost *desperate* about it. "I wanted to talk to you."

"About what?"

Eden held out her cell phone with his text message still on it. "About us."

"There is no us."

"Don't you think texting me was a little cold?" she asked. "Why couldn't you call me?"

Keith walked around Eden and opened his locker, taking off his navy blue parka and hanging it inside. "I don't know."

"Why are you breaking up with me?"

Keith started removing some textbooks. "It's over. Why can't you accept it?"

"Because I want to know why. Don't I deserve that? I have feelings for you and I thought you had feelings for me."

"Well, I don't."

Ouch! That stung! "Did you ever?" Eden wasn't sure if she wanted to hear his answer, but she had to know.

Keith shrugged. "We went out on a couple of dates. We kissed a few times. It's not like we were a couple. Why are you making this into something bigger than it was?"

Eden shook her phone in his face. "Because this message came out of nowhere. The last time I saw you, on Saturday night, when you kissed me good night on my front porch, I thought I still had a boyfriend. But then I figured something might be up when you weren't answering my calls and texts since Sunday. I'm not clueless. What's going on?"

Keith slammed his locker door shut. "I'm just not that into you anymore."

"Who are you into?" Eden asked. "That girl I saw you with in the cafeteria yesterday?"

A guilty look washed over Keith's face.

Gotcha! Eden thought.

"You coward!" she exclaimed. "You didn't have the guts to tell me that you were dumping me for another girl. It's not that you're not *into* me anymore. It's that you're *more* into her!"

Keith didn't deny it and Eden could feel the tears building in the corners of her eyes. She shoved past Keith and hurried down the hallway. She was *not* going to cry in front of him! If he didn't want to be with her anymore, fine. She deserved to be with a guy who wanted to be with her.

But even though she knew all this, it still hurt that Keith had chosen to be with another girl.

* * *

"What am I going to wear on my date on Saturday night?" Jennifer asked Violet as they walked to school.

"Date? What date?"

"With Will!"

"It's *not* a date," Violet sternly reminded her. "You're going to a party together. Besides, it's not like he's your *real* boyfriend. You don't have to impress the guy. You can wear whatever you want."

"I have to make it look like I've put *some* effort into it."

"Why?"

Jennifer laughed. "What?"

"It sounds like you care what Will thinks about you. And that can only mean one thing. Trouble." Violet pulled Jennifer onto a bench in front of a coffee shop. "We need to talk."

"About what?" Jennifer asked, noticing the serious expression on Violet's face.

"This situation. I'm getting worried."

"Situation?"

"You've got to guard your heart," Violet warned. "Even though this is all pretend, you're going to be spending a lot of time with Will."

"And?"

"You need to be careful that you don't really fall for him."

Jennifer laughed, getting off the bench and starting to walk again. "That'll never happen!"

"Why not?" Violet asked, hurrying after her. "What about all those girls he's gone out with and never called back? It happened to them! There's a reason why he's called the Heartbreaker and I don't want you finding out!"

"I'm different from those other girls," Jennifer said as she waited at a corner for the stoplight to change from red to green.

"How?" Violet demanded, catching up with her.

"Easy," Jennifer answered. "I'm not going to fall for him. And I know that after Valentine's Day, Will and I will go our separate ways."

"Well, I'm still going to be keeping my eye on you," Violet said. "Just to be on the safe side."

"You're overreacting. There's nothing to worry about. You'll see."

Violet didn't answer.

"Violet?"

"I think you have something to worry about," Violet said, pointing across the street at the North Ridge High student parking lot.

Jennifer followed Violet's pointing finger and couldn't believe what she was seeing. Will had just parked his motorcycle. That wasn't the problem. The problem was the girl sitting behind him with her arms wrapped snugly around his waist! Jennifer watched as she jumped off the back of the motorcycle, handed Will her helmet — tossing out her long, sun-streaked blonde, shampoo-commercial perfect hair — and then hurried into the school.

When the stoplight changed to green, Jennifer rushed across the parking lot to Will's side.

"What do you think you're doing?" she shrieked, confronting him like a crazy girl, throwing her arms up in the air.

"Hey, Jessica!" Will took off his motorcycle helmet and ran a gloved hand through his hair, unmussing it. His blue eyes were hidden behind his mirrored sunglasses. "How's it going?"

"My name's not Jessica!"

"It isn't?" Will held up a hand. "Wait, don't tell me. Let me think. Jenna? Jillian? Jane?"

"It's Jennifer!" she hissed.

Will slammed a hand against his forehead. "Jennifer! Right! Sorry. I forgot. But I knew it started with a *J*."

Jennifer couldn't tell if Will had really forgotten her name or if he was only messing around with her. She'd worry about that later.

"We're supposed to be a couple!" she reminded him. "Did you forget that?"

Will took off his sunglasses, tucking them into a pocket of his motorcycle jacket. He smiled at Jennifer, his ice blue eyes filled with amusement. "What are you having a meltdown about?"

"That girl!"

"What about her?"

"You gave her a ride on your motorcycle."

"So?"

"She looked pretty cozy sitting behind you! What's everyone going to think if my boyfriend is giving a ride to another girl? They're going to think he's cheating on me!"

"Nice to know you have such faith in me," Will said.

"You do have a reputation," Violet piped up as she joined them. "No offense. I'm just saying."

"I'm well aware of my so-called reputation," Will said to Violet. "I don't need you reminding me."

Violet blushed with embarrassment before turning to Jennifer. "I'll see you inside."

g a ride to is my next-
explained after Violet
;. I've given her rides
eed to control that jeal-

ınifer quickly snapped.
"

ısually have pet names
face matches your red

"

› in surrender. "Touchy,

r students were staring
ey walked through the
they hadn't heard what
s obvious that she and

us," Jennifer whispered.
o?"

'e to do something!
to talk about us."
ɜood thing that they saw

·anicked Jennifer asked.

"We were having a fight," Will pointed out. "That's what couples do, right? They fight. It means they've got a lot of passion for each other. And passion equals love."

Will's answer left Jennifer speechless. But before she could answer, he gave her a quick wink and headed into school.

Mindy Yee was waiting to pounce when Eden walked into the school library.

"Eden!" Mindy exclaimed, abandoning her notebook and rushing to Eden's side, steering her to the empty chair next to hers at the table where she was studying. "I heard all about your breakup with Keith! How are you doing?"

Mindy Yee was the last person Eden wanted to talk to. Mindy was the biggest gossip at North Ridge High. Eden knew that if she told Mindy anything, the entire school would know it all by the end of the day. Not that she would. She didn't consider Mindy a friend. The person she really wanted to talk to was Natalie, but she wouldn't be able to do that until lunch.

"Who told you that Keith and I broke up?" The question slipped out before she could stop herself. Other than Claudia, she hadn't discussed it with anyone.

"Deena told me."

"Deena?"

Mindy's almond-shaped eyes glittered with excitement as she dropped her bombshell, waiting to see Eden's reaction. "Keith's new girlfriend."

Miss Braids, Eden thought. Obviously she knew who to talk to. No one spread the dirt faster than Mindy.

"Is it true that he didn't break up with you in person?" Mindy asked, trying to look sympathetic. "That he sent you a text message?"

Eden wanted to ask Mindy why she was asking the question since it was obvious Deena had told her everything. Instead, she got out of her seat. "Mindy, I'm sure you know how painful breakups can be." She was sure Mindy *didn't*. She couldn't remember the last time a guy had gone out with this blabbermouth. "It's too personal to discuss."

Then Eden left the table before Mindy could say anything else, searching for her tutor. As she did, she ran into Lily Norris, who worked part-time at the library.

"I couldn't help but overhear Mindy," Lily said. "I'd love to strangle her! Why can't she mind her own business? If it's any consolation, I know exactly what you're going through."

Eden remembered that Lily used to date Jason Fitzpatrick. Their first date had been last year at the Valentine's Day dance. They had dated for most of the spring, but when Jason had gone away for the summer to work at a sleepaway camp, he had met another girl and broken up with Lily via e-mail.

"I guess getting dumped by e-mail is just as bad as getting dumped with a text message," Eden said.

"Breakups suck, no matter how they happen," Lily said. "It hurts at first, but then the hurt goes away. Just give yourself some time. Don't give up. The right guy is waiting. No one knows that better than me."

Eden knew Lily had met her boyfriend Simon in December during the Secret Santa exchange. There had been a lot of misunderstandings between the two of them, because of the Secret Santa game, but eventually they'd wound up together.

Eden gave Lily a smile. "Thanks."

After Lily returned to the front desk, Eden sat herself down at a table in the back and pulled out her SAT study guide. She was familiarizing herself with a bunch of different vocabulary words when her tutor, Dexter King, arrived.

When Eden's parents decided she needed a tutor, Eden had gone to the school guidance office. In addition to the private tutor she met with at home every Saturday morning, the school had assigned Dexter, one of the smartest guys in her junior class, to work with her. They met three times a week during her free period. While Claudia and Natalie were hanging out in the cafeteria doing homework or just gossiping during their free period, she was stuck with Dexter. It wasn't that she didn't like Dexter. She just couldn't wait until the SATs were over and she could get her free time back.

If Eden had to use one word to describe Dexter, it would be *preppy*. Every day he always wore the same thing: khaki pants, burgundy penny loafers, a white (or blue) Oxford shirt, and either a pullover sweater or a vest. He was tall and lanky, his skin was the color of mocha, and his brown hair was short and spiky.

"Have you been crying?" Dexter asked, pulling his book bag over his head.

"Is it that obvious?" Eden asked in a panic, reaching into her shoulder bag for her compact and checking her face. She'd popped into the girls' bathroom between classes. Her eyes had been a little swollen during first period but she thought they had gone back to normal the last time she had checked.

"No," he said, taking the seat across from her and pulling out his SAT study guide. "But your eyes are sad. Did something happen?"

"My boyfriend broke up with me." Eden sniffed. "I might as well tell you how he broke up with me since I'm sure the entire school is going to know by the end of today. He sent me a text message."

"That's cold."

"I know." Eden could feel the tears coming back, but she fought them off. She was *not* going to cry in front of Mindy Yee! She could see her at her table, craning her neck like a vulture, trying to figure out what was going on between her and Dexter. "And now his new girlfriend is making sure everyone knows what he did."

"Well, just ignore it. You've got more important stuff to worry about."

"Like what?"

Dexter held up his SAT study guide. "Like this."

Dexter turned to the vocabulary section and began reading off a list. But every word he quizzed Eden on, she got wrong. After ten minutes, he closed the study guide.

"You're not concentrating."

"I'm sorry, but I can't," Eden wailed. "I keep thinking about Keith and Miss Braids."

"Miss Braids?"

"Deena!" Eden spat out. "His new girlfriend." A thought suddenly occurred to Eden. "I bet it was her idea to have Keith text me! Oooh, she better hide the next time she sees me because I'm going to yank every single one of those braids out of her head!"

"Why are you letting them get to you this way?" Dexter asked. "Okay, Keith dumped you. And maybe his new girlfriend helped him. They're nasty and they deserve each other. You deserve better."

"I do?"

"Yes, you do. But you can't sit around feeling sorry for yourself."

Dexter began packing up his bag.

"Where are you going?" Eden asked.

"We're not going to get anything done this morning," he said, pulling his book bag back over his head. "Why don't we meet after school and try again? Maybe by then you'll have gotten this out of your system."

"Out of my system?" Eden snapped in disbelief. She couldn't believe what she was hearing! "Have you ever been in love?"

Dexter shook his head. "No, I haven't."

Eden pointed a finger at Dexter's chest. "Until you do, don't tell me what I *should* and *shouldn't* be feeling. It's not easy getting over a broken heart!"

Then Eden gathered her books and stormed out of the library.

Chapter Six

"We need to go to the mall after school," Claudia announced as she sat across from Natalie and Eden in the cafeteria.

"We do?" Natalie asked. "Why?"

"Shopping! Not only do I want to buy a new outfit for my party on Saturday night, but I want to find a dress for the Valentine's Day dance. We've only got a week to shop and if we don't find anything at the mall, then I want to go into Manhattan this weekend."

Natalie popped a straw into her can of Diet Pepsi. "Any idea what kind of dress you want?"

Claudia shook her head. "I just want it to be pink."

Natalie vaguely recalled Claudia saying something the day before about wanting a pink dress but she couldn't remember why. Half the time, she tuned Claudia out, which was risky, since you didn't want Claudia to think you weren't hanging on to her every word. Natalie decided to take a chance. "Pink? How come?"

"Pink is the perfect color for Valentine's Day."

"Don't mention that day to me," Eden moaned as she took a bite of her grilled cheese sandwich.

Claudia turned to Natalie. "What's wrong with her?"

Eden pushed away her sandwich. "In case you've forgotten, I've been dumped!"

Claudia opened a bag of barbecue potato chips. "Are you still boo-hooing over it? Please! It's time to move on!"

"Claudia!" Natalie exclaimed, putting an arm around Eden and giving her a hug. "Can't you be more sensitive? Eden's hurting."

"And whose fault is that?" Claudia bit into a potato chip and started crunching. "Are you going to mope around because Keith broke your heart? He's not worth it. That's why you have to come shopping with me this afternoon."

"I do?" Eden asked.

Claudia nodded wisely. "The best revenge

is looking hot. Plus, it'll help you find a new boyfriend."

"I'm through with dating," Eden vowed.

Claudia laughed. "You say that now. But you'll go running the next time a hunky jock flexes his muscles at you. Wait and see."

Eden stared at Claudia in disbelief. "Are you saying I'm superficial? That I only care about what a guy looks like?"

Claudia began counting off on her fingers. "Let's see. Keith was on the basketball team. Luther was on the baseball team. Malcolm was on the football team. What did they all have in common? Muscles, muscles, and more muscles."

"That's not my fault," Eden snapped. "I'm a cheerleader! We ride the same bus with the guys to the games. It's how we got to know each other."

"Enough with the jocks!" Claudia exclaimed, opening a bottle of peach Snapple and taking a sip. "You need to start looking elsewhere for dating material. The mall is the perfect place!"

"You have a point," Eden grudgingly agreed. "But I can't go today."

"How come?"

"I rescheduled my tutoring session with Dexter for after school."

Claudia turned to Natalie. "I guess it's just you and me."

Natalie shook her head. "I can't go either."

Claudia pouted. "Why not?"

"I promised my neighbor Lisa that I'd babysit Bonnie."

"Ugh! How can you stand being around that rug rat again? My ears are still ringing from all that wailing she did yesterday afternoon."

"It didn't last very long." Of course, that was because of Leo. Natalie hoped that Bonnie didn't decide to throw another tantrum once her mother left the house.

As if reading her mind, Claudia said, "Better remember to bring a set of earplugs."

Jennifer was busy working on her Most Romantic Couple essay when a voice asked, "Is this seat taken?"

She looked up and saw Will standing above her with a lunch tray.

"What do you want?" she asked in surprise.

"Is that any way to greet your boyfriend?"

id into the seat opposite
d a ham-and-cheese hero.
ould be seen having lunch
are dating."
oss the table. "Go away!
to know about us until

is hero and started talking
Why's that?"
Will's shoulder and across
le where Claudia was sit-
hem. "I want the element
n't going to expect me to
you."
ifer's gaze. "Relax. She
to popular belief, not all
ne back of their heads."
s joke. "Still, you should
safe side."
kick?"
, she's in the library study-
n American History next

pages in Jennifer's hand.
g on?"

"Our essay?"

"For the Most Romantic Couple contest," she explained.

"Mind if I take a look?"

Jennifer grudgingly handed over the pages she'd been working on. "It's very rough," she warned him. "I still have to polish it up."

She watched as Will read the pages. From the face he was making, she could see he didn't like them.

"What's wrong?" she asked in a panic.

"It's so, so . . ." Will struggled to find the right word. "Ooey-gooey. And sappy!"

"Don't you mean sweet and romantic?"

"No, I mean ooey-gooey. You're giving me sugar shock! We met on New Year's Eve and I asked if I could give you your first kiss of the new year?"

"I already told Claudia that, so it has to be part of our story."

"We talk on the phone every night? We like snuggling on the couch watching TV? We go to pet shops and look at the puppies in the window, giving them names? We like walking through the snow holding hands?" Will gagged. "This isn't me!"

"Then who are you?" Jennifer asked.

"You tell me," Will challenged.

"Fine," Jennifer said. "You're a bad boy. You like breaking the rules. You like doing your own thing and not answering to anyone else. You like shocking people and catching them off guard. You never expected to go out with a 'good' girl like me. You only go out with girls who are as bad as you."

"That's an urban myth. I go out with lots of nice girls."

"But you only go out with them *once*," Jennifer reminded him.

Will shook his head. "That's not true. Sometimes I go out with them twice. Same with the so-called *bad* girls, who really aren't so bad, just so you know."

"You're hard to figure out," Jennifer continued. "You don't want anyone to get too close, so you keep them at a distance."

"What's so hard? I'd rather hang out with my friends, do my own thing. I don't need some girl constantly harping at me, asking me where I am, where I'm going, telling me when to call her and freaking out if I forget. I already have a mother. I don't need another one."

"Do you think all girls are like that?"

"I don't think *you* are."

"You don't?" Jennifer was surprised.

Will shook his head. "Nope. I think you're your own person. Look at the way you're standing up to Claudia. You're not sucking up to her the way everyone else does. You're not afraid of her the way they are. I like that."

"You do?"

"Sure. It takes guts."

"Either that or stupidity," Jennifer admitted. "I'm still not sure which."

"And you don't need to be defined by the person you're dating. I don't see you as the clingy type. You don't have to be Will's Girlfriend. If anything, you're the kick-butt type! That's why we're attracted to each other. We do our own thing and we respect that. We're not trying to change each other. And because we've just started going out, we're still learning about each other and that's the most romantic thing of all. Because we keep discovering how much we have in common." Will leaned back in his seat, giving Jennifer a smug smile. "There's your essay."

Jennifer hated to admit it, but it was good. *Very* good. It was simple and honest and straight

:umpled up the essay she
d began writing furiously

reful," she warned him.
ıave gotten ourselves a

ıe day ended, Eden headed

the table where she and
:d, she found a surprise

lips.
l with a yellow ribbon and
two words printed on it:

lips put a smile on Eden's
n could have left her the

arted wondering. Did he
ether with her? Why else
the tulips?
er thoughts, trying to fig-
vers meant, when Dexter
ext to her. "Before we get

started, I just want to say I'm sorry if I hurt your feelings this morning," he said. "I was being insensitive. I should have been more aware of what you're going through. It can't be fun going through a breakup. I hope you'll forgive me."

Poor Dexter! He looked so serious. Like he was afraid that she was going to snap at him again. If anyone was owed an apology, it was him. He'd been the target of all her anger this morning. She'd been mad at Keith. At Deena. Even at Mindy. And she'd taken it all out on him.

"I'll forgive you if you forgive me," she said. "I wasn't so nice myself. Deal?"

Dexter gave Eden a smile. "Deal." He pointed to the bouquet she was holding. "I see you found the tulips."

Eden held out the bouquet. "Aren't they pretty?"

"I wasn't sure if you'd like them."

Eden stared at Dexter in shock. She couldn't have heard him correctly. "What did you say?"

"I said I wasn't sure if you'd like them."

"*You* left me the tulips?"

"Yes. Why? Who did you think they were from?" As soon as the words were out of Dexter's mouth, realization dawned on him. "You thought they were from Keith. Oh, Eden. I'm so sorry. I wasn't thinking."

"That's okay. It's not your fault," she assured him, fighting against the devastation she felt. Keith *wasn't* sorry. He *didn't* want to get back together with her. He was still with Deena. "You were trying to do something nice for me. It's not your fault that I jumped to conclusions."

Eden stared at the tulips. Now that she knew they were from Dexter, they weren't as special as they had seemed. She pushed them to one side and pulled out her SAT exam book.

"Are you sure you're okay?" Dexter asked. "I feel awful. I didn't mean to upset you."

"I'm fine," Eden insisted. "Really. Start quizzing me."

As Dexter started asking her vocabulary words, Eden wondered if her day could get any worse.

Right now, all she wanted was for it to be over.

Once she was finished with Dexter, she was going to go home, get into bed, pull the covers over her head, and cry her eyes out.

Chapter Seven

The smell of tomato sauce and garlic was heavy in the air as Jennifer walked into Marinelli's Pizzeria. She inhaled deeply and heard her stomach rumbling.

"Can I get you a slice?" Will asked from behind the counter. He stared at her stomach. "Sounds like you're hungry."

Jennifer blushed in embarrassment. "I'll have a slice."

"Pepperoni and mushroom?"

"Plain is fine," she said as she reached into her shoulder bag for her wallet.

"Keep your money," Will said. "It's on me."

"Thanks."

"Why don't you grab a corner table? I'll be with you in a couple of minutes."

As Jennifer waited for Will, she looked around the pizzeria. It was warm and cozy, decorated to look like it was actually in Italy. The walls were made of brick and they were strung with tiny white lights. The tables were covered with red and white checked tablecloths and on top of them were melted candles stuck in wine bottles. There was an Italian flag hanging on one wall and posters of Italian soccer players on another.

Jennifer watched as Will twirled a ball of pizza dough around one hand. It kept getting bigger and bigger until it was a flat circle. Then he placed it back down on the marble countertop, tossed some flour on it, added a swirl of tomato sauce with a big spoon, and sprinkled a handful of mozzarella. Then he slid a wooden spatula underneath the pizza and popped it into one of the four ovens behind him.

Jennifer left her seat and walked over to the counter. "I didn't know you made the pizzas."

"I'm a guy of many talents." Will opened one of the other ovens and pulled out Jennifer's slice. "Here you go. Piping hot."

Jennifer blew onto the slice so she wouldn't burn her mouth and then took a tiny bite. "Mmm. Good!"

"Want to try making one?" Will asked.

"How hard is it?" Jennifer asked, taking another bite of her slice.

"You won't know until you try."

Jennifer studied Will. "If you can do it, I can do it!"

Will laughed. "We'll see! It's not as easy as it looks."

Jennifer stepped behind the counter next to Will and tried to imitate what she had seen him do earlier. But she was unable to twirl the ball of dough covering her hand. It was so heavy! It kept falling off her hand with a thud, scattering flour everywhere.

"Can't I just flatten it out with a rolling pin?" she asked.

"You're making a pizza pie, not an apple pie!" Will stood behind Jennifer, holding her arm straight. "You're concentrating too much. Just go with the flow. Little twirls. As you keep doing it, the dough will start to grow and stretch." Will began turning Jennifer's arm. "Pretend you're twirling a hula hoop around your wrist."

Jennifer tried again and this time the ball of dough began to grow. "I'm doing it!" she exclaimed.

"Keep twirling," Will encouraged.

Jennifer tried to focus on her twirling, but it was hard with Will standing so close to her. The space behind the counter was small and she could sense him right behind her.

"Very good," he whispered in her ear.

Chills traveled down Jennifer's spine and she shivered. For a second, she wondered if Will was going to touch her, but he didn't. Instead, he stepped away to wait on a customer and left her to twirling her dough. When she had a circle as big as the one Will had made, she added the other ingredients. As she did, she watched Will talking to the girl on the other side of the counter. She was the same age as them, but Jennifer didn't recognize her from school. It was obvious that she was interested in more than just a slice of pizza. She kept batting her eyes at Will and asking him all sorts of meaningless questions. She was flirting with Will and he was flirting right back!

When she paid, the girl wrote her phone number down on a piece of paper and slipped it into the front pocket of Will's shirt. "Call me," she said.

Will gave her a smile. "I love making home deliveries."

Will watched the girl leave the pizzeria before turning back to Jennifer. "How's your pie coming?"

Jennifer stared at Will in disbelief. She couldn't believe what she had just seen!

"What was that?" she demanded.

"What?" Will innocently asked.

Jennifer reached into Will's pocket and pulled out the girl's number, waving it in his face. "This!" she proclaimed before shredding the slip of paper and tossing the pieces into the garbage.

"Hey!" Will protested. "What did you do that for?"

"In case you've forgotten, you now have a girlfriend," she reminded him. "*Me!* Your days of playing the field are over."

"I wasn't going to call her." Will crossed his heart and gave Jennifer a sweet smile. "I swear."

Jennifer was tempted to peek behind Will's back to see if he was crossing his fingers. Oooh, he was good. A natural-born charmer. Always ready with a smile. He knew how to wrap girls around his little finger, but she wasn't going to be one of those girls!

"If I flirt with the girls, they tip me better," Will explained. "What's wrong with that?"

"You need to tone it down."

"We've discussed your jealousy, Red." Will shook his head sadly. "Not very attractive."

"I am *not* jealous!" Jennifer exclaimed. "And don't call me Red!"

"You don't have anything to worry about," he reassured her. "Until February fifteenth, I'm all yours."

Jennifer wanted to scream. He was *so* infuriating!

"What's not sinking into that thick skull of yours?" she asked. "What I just saw makes it look like you were interested in that girl. And if *I* think that, then other people are going to think it, too."

"You mean Claudia?"

"Yes!"

Will popped Jennifer's pizza into the oven and led her back to the table she had been sitting at.

"Okay, no more flirting," he said. "I promise. I want this plan to work just as much as you do. Tell me again about New Year's Eve and our first kiss."

Jennifer gave Will a recap of what she had told Claudia the day before.

"What was the kiss like?" Will asked.

His question caught Jennifer off guard. "Huh?"

"Our kiss. What was it like? How did it feel?"

Jennifer shrugged. "I don't know."

"Don't you think you should? In case she asks."

"I-I-I suppose," Jennifer sputtered.

"We need to work on that," Will said firmly. "Maybe even practice. You know. Like research. So it feels real and you know what you're talking about." Will popped a piece of gum into his mouth, smiling at Jennifer while he chewed. "Don't worry, my breath is always minty fresh."

"R-r-research?" Jennifer asked, suddenly feeling like Little Red Riding Hood standing in front of the Big Bad Wolf.

"Do you have a problem with that? Obviously, if we're a couple, we're going to need to be affectionate with each other. Right?"

Jennifer hated to admit it, but none of this was stuff she had thought about.

"Right?" Will repeated.

"Right," Jennifer answered firmly. So they

were going to eventually kiss. Not a problem. It was all part of the plan.

"But we don't have to worry about that now," Will said. "Let's get back to New Year's Eve. I was home sick that night so your story works. In fact, I had the flu during the holiday break and pretty much stayed home the entire time."

"Bummer."

"What did you do?"

"We visited my cousins in Pennsylvania and went skiing. We could say we met at the party that the ski lodge had on New Year's Eve. They really did have one."

"What about afterward? Why haven't we been seen out together? You know she's going to wonder about that."

"We wanted to take things slow," Jennifer said. "Get to know each other. I was afraid."

"Afraid? Of what?"

"I didn't want to be another one-time-only date. I fell hard for you, but I wanted to see how serious you were about me."

"And am I serious?" Will asked, leaning back in his chair and stretching out his legs.

"You tell me," Jennifer said. "Have you been dating anyone since New Year's Eve?"

"Lucky for you, I haven't."

"What do you like to do for fun?"

"I've got my motorcycle. I listen to music. Play video games. Go to concerts. Work here. Pretty much the same as any other seventeen-year-old guy."

Jennifer handed Will a sheet of paper.

"What's this?" he asked, looking it over.

"It's all about me," she explained. "My birthday, my favorite color, favorite foods, foods I hate, favorite movies, favorite bands, favorite TV shows, the names of my cat and best friend. Memorize it. I'll need you to do a list for me and the sooner the better. We've only got tomorrow and Saturday afternoon to get ready."

"That's like homework!"

"Do you want this to work or don't you? We're going to have a tough time trying to fool Claudia. We have to have our stories straight."

"Okay, okay," Will grumbled. "I hear you."

"When can you get me a list?"

"Why don't you stick around this afternoon and take notes?"

Jennifer pulled out her cell phone and checked the time. "I wish I could, but I've got to get to my part-time job."

ore. I'm stuck in
only do I have to
their stressed-out

nere long?"
s like forever. And
't think I'm ever
's too much work.

ll said, studying
I bet you'd make a

open. Where had

ks beautiful," Will
it's her special day.
have you?"
No, I haven't." She
get going."
ront door of the piz-
Red! Wait!"
Will hurried up to
He started to lean
he thought he was
heart began racing
at her cheek and

held out his fingers. "You had some flour on your face."

Disappointment washed over Jennifer. Had she really thought he was going to kiss her?

"What's wrong?" Will asked. "You look upset."

Jennifer scowled. "I told you not to call me Red!"

And then she stomped out of the pizzeria.

"If you won't come shopping with me, I'll bring the shopping to you!"

Claudia walked into the Barneses' house with four garment bags.

"What are those?" Natalie asked as she followed Claudia into the living room, weaving around a path of toys. She'd have to clean up before Lisa came home.

"Possibilities for the Valentine's Day dance," Claudia said. "I need a second opinion."

Bonnie, who was playing with her Barbies, abandoned them and came running over to Claudia's side.

"Pretty," she whispered as she watched Claudia unzip the bags and remove the shiny, sparkly dresses inside. "Like a princess."

se?" Natalie asked in dis-
n the couch and lifting

ey're all on loan because
from this boutique."
a fashion show," Natalie
disappeared into the first-
ge.
laimed, happily clapping
to an opened box of choc-
e. "May I have one?"
talie opened the box and
'Just one. Because you've

had been no temper tan-
ft that afternoon. Bonnie
good-bye and gone off to
leaving Natalie to do her

chocolates, squishing three
the one she wanted. She
when Claudia returned
It was an off-the-shoulder
nk cotton candy. Bonnie's
when she saw it.
k?" Claudia asked, twirl-

"It's nice," Natalie said.

"Can I try it on?" Bonnie asked. "Pleeeease?"

"It's too big for you," Natalie said as Claudia disappeared to change into her second dress.

Seven dresses later Claudia still hadn't picked one to wear for the dance.

She plopped on the couch next to Natalie. "I like all of them, but I don't *love* any of them."

"You're pretty," Bonnie said, wrapping her arms around Claudia's neck and giving her a kiss on the cheek, leaving behind a chocolate lipstick mark.

"Is she always so sticky?" Claudia asked, touching her cheek.

"She's a little girl! She's allowed to be messy. She doesn't have to be all perfect the way we do." Natalie lifted Bonnie off the couch. "Let's go wash your hands and face."

"I'm hardly perfect," Claudia said as she followed after them. "But I will be the night of the Valentine's Day dance."

Natalie squirted Bonnie's hands with liquid soap. Then she turned on the water, adjusting the knobs until it was warm. "Start scrubbing," she told her. Bonnie instantly began lathering up.

"Have you bought a dress for the dance yet?" Claudia asked.

ıtly wiped it
I'm sure I'll

ɛ's expecting

with a towel,
her hands.

uss it with
pointing out
:hen suggest-
taste ran to
clines, which
ɛ wore some-
e a point of
ıer.
ɛmember the
Secret Santa

ht you'd look

was strapless
:aring a dress
: dance."

"Tom doesn't like Tanya. He likes you."

Does he? Natalie felt like asking. Because lately she'd been wondering.

"Can you unzip me?" Claudia asked, turning her back around to Natalie. "I'm going to take these dresses back to the mall."

"We'll go with you," Natalie said. "Bonnie's been such a good girl today that I promised to take her sledding in the park."

"Sledding! Yay!" Bonnie shrieked, running off to find her snow boots.

Natalie watched Bonnie disappear, wondering what it would be like to be that young again and not have to worry about life in high school.

At the park, Bonnie insisted on giving Claudia a kiss good-bye. Natalie watched with amusement as Bonnie gave Claudia a bunch of extra wet, extra slobbery kisses all over her face. Even though Claudia tried not to cringe, she did, and Natalie laughed.

"Stop acting like a baby!" Natalie scolded as she watched Claudia pull a tissue out of her pocket. "It wasn't that bad!"

"My face is dripping wet," she said, wiping it off. "If I don't dry it, it'll freeze."

Natalie said as she took
er to one of the highest

" she asked when they

d.
the sled and positioned
. When her legs were
waist, she pushed them
med with delight as they

nie cried when the sled

lown again we're going
vay up." Natalie pointed
e down. "Can you walk
iin?"
ave her a ride on their

d. "Uncle Leo!"
ed. "You look so yummy.
ou!" He scooped Bonnie
ended to eat her arm.

nie giggled. "Please!"
back down on the

ground. "Okay. But only because you said the magic word."

"Hi, Leo," Natalie said.

"Hey, Natalie. What are you two doing here?"

"I'm babysitting Bonnie again. Because she was so good, I told her I'd take her sledding."

"Did you have fun going down the hill?" Leo asked Bonnie, who instantly nodded.

"You know what else is fun?"

"What?"

"Building a snowman. Want to help me?"

Bonnie raced to Natalie's side. "Can we help Uncle Leo build a snowman, Natalie? Can we? *Please?*"

"If that's what you want to do, sure."

"Have you ever built one of these before?" Leo asked Natalie as he began building a base for the snowman's bottom.

Natalie shook her head. "Have you?"

"Nope."

"How hard could it be? All we have to do is make three big snowballs and plop them on top of each other."

An hour later they had built a lopsided snowman with two gray rocks for eyes and a gnarled tree branch for a nose. A brown leaf had been added for a mouth and icicles were sticking out of his head for hair.

"How come it doesn't look like the snowmen on TV?" Leo asked Natalie. "You know, all perfectly round and shiny white?"

"That is one sad-looking snowman," Natalie stated.

But Bonnie disagreed.

"He's the most beautiful snowman in the whole wide world," she declared.

"What are we going to name it?" Leo asked.

"Frosty!" Bonnie pronounced.

"It's her favorite DVD," Leo whispered to Natalie.

"I know. She watched it four times this afternoon."

"You got off easy. Whenever I babysit her, she watches it at least ten times. If I have to hear that stupid snowman say 'Happy Birthday' one more time, I'll scream!"

"I still have to take her back home, so I'm sure we'll be watching it again." Natalie noticed that it was starting to get dark and held her hand out to Bonnie. "It's time to go."

"Can Uncle Leo come with us?" Bonnie asked as she slipped one red mittened hand inside of Natalie's and the other inside of Leo's.

"If he wants to." Natalie looked at Leo. "Were you going anywhere before you ran into us?"

"Just on my way home from the school library. I was working on my term paper for English Lit."

"Who do you have?" Natalie asked as they started walking out of the park.

"O'Callahan."

"I hear she's supposed to be tough."

"She's not so bad if you read the assignments."

"Uncle Leo, will you read me a book when we get home?" Bonnie asked.

"Absolutely!" Leo promised.

When they got home from the park, Natalie changed Bonnie into a dry pair of jeans and socks. Bonnie insisted on wearing her purple jeans, which clashed with her orange turtleneck. And she wanted to wear her green and yellow striped socks.

"Yowza!" Leo exclaimed, covering his eyes when Bonnie returned to the living room. "Dig those crazy colors!"

"They're not crazy, they're my favorites."

Leo held out two books. "Which one do you want me to read? *Fancy Nancy* or *Knuffle Bunny*?"

Bonnie shook her head. "I don't want to read a book. I want to watch a DVD."

"Which one?" Natalie and Leo asked at the same time.

"*Frosty the Snowman*!"

"Wouldn't you rather watch *The Little Mermaid*?" Natalie asked.

"No."

"*Beauty and the Beast*?" Leo suggested.

"No."

"How about *Cinderella*?" Natalie offered.

Bonnie stomped her foot and screwed up her face, taking in a deep breath as she got ready to scream. "NO! I . . . WANT . . . TO . . . WATCH . . . FROSTY!"

"Okay, okay, *Frosty* it is!" Natalie said, hurrying to aim the remote control at the DVD player. Anything to avoid a tantrum.

Bonnie nestled into a corner of the couch, popping her thumb into her mouth and snuggling with a baby doll.

"Why don't I make us some popcorn?" Leo suggested, heading into the kitchen. "You can't watch a movie without popcorn."

"I like my popcorn plain," Natalie called out as she started picking up Bonnie's toys. "No butter."

"No butter," Leo called back.

Natalie had just finished collecting the last of Bonnie's toys when the doorbell rang. Opening the front door, she was surprised to see Tom standing on the porch.

"What are you doing here?" she exclaimed as he stepped inside.

"Tracking you down."

She closed the door behind him. "Why?"

"We had a study date tonight, remember?"

Natalie clasped a hand over her mouth. "I forgot!" she gasped.

"Obviously."

She could see he was mad from the way he was glowering at her, but she chose to ignore it. She'd made a mistake. What was the big deal? "How did you know I was here?"

"Your mother told me."

"Natalie, who's at the door?"

Leo walked out of the kitchen with a big bowl of popcorn.

"Having a little snack, Barnes?" Tom snickered.

Natalie noticed that at the sight of Tom, Leo seemed to shrink into himself. Why wouldn't he? Tom was usually one of the guys who laughed at Leo.

Tom turned back to Natalie. "What's he doing

ere babysitting some little
again. "What's the mat-
nd Daddy won't leave you
the only way you can get

Bonnie," Natalie said,
ments. "She's four years
He stopped by to drop off

why she was lying. She
t if Tom knew she had
vith Leo, he wouldn't be
he tried to communicate
er eyes. *Please back me*

led.
ng out of the living room.
build another snowman

talie?" Bonnie asked.
nswer, Tom did for her.
to be busy tomorrow

er. "Oh, I am?"
n insisted.

If there was one thing Natalie hated, it was someone telling her what to do. But she wasn't about to get into a fight with Tom in front of Leo.

"Let's go watch *Frosty*," Leo said, taking Bonnie's hand in his.

"What are you doing hanging out with that loser?" Tom asked after Leo had disappeared.

"Leo's not a loser!"

"You could have fooled me! He definitely looks like one!"

"Not everyone can look like they stepped out of the pages of *Sports Illustrated*," Natalie snapped.

"They can if they exercise and don't eat like a pig."

"Lower your voice!"

"Why? It's the truth. It's not my fault if the truth hurts." Tom raised his voice. "I bet he's scarfed down that entire bowl of popcorn. Going back for seconds, Barnes?"

"Why are you being so mean? What did Leo ever do to you?"

Tom took Natalie by the hand. "Let's get out of here. We've got studying to do."

Natalie snatched away her hand. "I can't. I'm babysitting Bonnie."

"Can't Leo do it? She's his niece. I'm sure he doesn't have anything better to do tonight. It's not like he has much of a social life."

Leo came back out into the hallway.

"Natalie, if you want to leave, you can," he offered. "I don't mind watching Bonnie."

"Let's go," Tom said, tugging on Natalie's arm. "Where's your coat?"

Natalie shook him off. "I can't leave."

"Why not? He said he'd watch the kid."

"That *kid* has a name. Bonnie. And she's my responsibility until Lisa returns home. She left her with *me*. Not Leo. Even though he's her uncle, I can't just walk out. That would be wrong."

Tom huffed.

Seconds later, headlights filled the driveway.

"Mommy's home!" Bonnie squealed, running out of the living room at the sound of a car pulling into the driveway.

"I guess you can go now," Tom said, walking out of the house. "I'll see you next door."

"Are you going home, Natalie?" Bonnie asked.

"Uh-huh."

"You're not going to get to have any popcorn with me and Uncle Leo." Bonnie's face became sad. "And you're not going to watch *Frosty* with us."

"We'll do it another time," Leo said, taking Bonnie by the hand and leading her back into the living room. "Right, Natalie?"

Natalie nodded. "Right. I promise."

Leo glanced at her over his shoulder. The look he gave her made her think he didn't believe her. But she had promised Bonnie and she wouldn't break her promise.

After Lisa came inside and paid her for watching Bonnie, Natalie slipped into her coat. From the living room, she could hear Leo talking along with Frosty while Bonnie giggled.

As she walked out the front door, Natalie suddenly felt sad and found herself wishing she could stay behind. The only place she wanted to be was sitting on the couch with Leo and Bonnie.

Chapter Eight

"But I don't want to see a horror movie!" Jennifer wailed. "I hate horror movies!"

It was Friday night, and Jennifer and Will were at the movie theater. That day Will had gotten detention for talking in Art class and Jennifer had had to work again, so they hadn't been able to get together after school. To make up for the lost time, Will had suggested they go to a movie and then hang out afterward.

Jennifer had come straight to the movie theater from DeVille's, so she hadn't had an opportunity to fix herself up. Not that she would have gone to a lot of effort if she'd come straight from home. After all, this wasn't a date. They were doing research!

She was wearing the same jeans and emerald

green pullover sweater she'd had on all day and her hair was in a ponytail. But before leaving DeVille's, she had popped into the cosmetics department to add a little lipstick and mascara and give herself a spritz of perfume. That's what free samples were for, right?

"How can you hate horror movies?" Will asked.

Jennifer began counting off on her fingers. "Blood. Guts. Gore. Screaming. Dead bodies. Creepy music. Crazy killers."

"Yeah! All the good stuff."

Jennifer shuddered. "Horror movies give me nightmares."

"Do you sleep with the light on after you've seen one?"

"If you want to know the truth, yes, I do," Jennifer admitted.

"Jennifer's afraid of the Boogeyman!" Will laughed. "Jennifer's afraid of the Boogeyman!"

Jennifer swatted him on the arm. "Shut up!" She pointed to the list of movies that were playing. "Why don't we see a nice romantic comedy? *Romancing Rachel* is supposed to be good."

Will stuck a finger down his throat. "Blech! I hate romantic comedies."

"Why? Afraid you might pick up some pointers?"

"Har. Har."

Jennifer checked the movie times. "We have to make a decision. The movies are going to start soon."

"Let's flip a coin," Will suggested. "Heads we see *The Next To Die* and tails we see *Romancing Rachel*. Deal?"

"Deal," Jennifer said, thinking that was fair.

Will reached into his pocket for a quarter. Then he tossed it in the air, caught it, and flipped it on the back of his hand.

"Yesss!" Will triumphantly exclaimed as he looked to see how the coin had landed. "We're going to see *The Next To Die*."

"Fine," Jennifer grumbled. "But here's a warning. I'm going to be clutching your arm throughout the entire movie."

Will stepped up to the ticket window. "Not a problem."

"Here's my money," Jennifer said, handing him some bills.

Will waved her money away. "Keep it. It's my treat."

"Thanks," she said. "But the munchies are on me."

At the refreshment stand, there was another round of arguing. "Let's get nachos," Will said.

Jennifer made a face. "Nachos? Who eats nachos at the movies?"

Will pointed to moviegoers who were heading back to their seats with nachos. "They do."

"Nachos aren't movie food!"

"Uh, look around. We're in a movie theater," Will pointed out. "And it's food."

"But it's not *movie* food!" Jennifer repeated.

"What's movie food?"

"Popcorn! It's been eaten at the movies for decades! Nachos haven't."

"But I like nachos," Will said.

"Those aren't *real* nachos like you'd get in a Mexican restaurant. The cheese here is made with some sort of artificial gunk." Jennifer shuddered. "Do you really want to be putting that in your stomach?"

"And the butter they put on the popcorn is real?" Will skeptically asked.

"I don't put butter on my popcorn," Jennifer shot back.

"Okay, forget the nachos. We'll have a bucket of popcorn."

"And some licorice," Jennifer told the girl behind the counter. "Red, please."

"Red? I like black."

Jennifer made a face. "I hate black licorice."

"I hate red licorice."

"Let's get M&M's instead," Jennifer said.

"What kind?" the girl behind the counter asked.

"Peanut," Jennifer said.

"Plain," Will said.

Jennifer turned to Will. "How can you not like peanut M&M's?"

"I like my chocolate to be pure."

"So you don't like Snickers bars?"

"Hate 'em."

"What's it going to be?" the girl asked in a bored voice.

"We'll take a box of each," Jennifer said.

The girl started ringing up their items. "Anything to drink?"

"I'll have a Pepsi," Will said.

"We don't sell Pepsi. Only Coke."

"I'll have a Coke," Jennifer said.

"Nothing for me," Will told the girl.

"Why won't you get a Coke?" Jennifer asked. "It's the same thing."

"No, it isn't."

"Now you're a soda connoisseur?"

"I can taste the difference," Will insisted.

"Whatever," Jennifer said as she paid the cashier.

Once they had their order, they headed into the movie theater. Most of the seats were taken, although they were a few empty spots scattered around. Will started walking to the front row.

"Where are you going?" Jennifer asked.

"To get our seats."

Jennifer shook her head. "I don't want to sit that close." She pointed to a row in the back. "Let's sit there."

"But it's so far away. We're hardly going to be able to see anything."

"Exactly! I don't need to be that close."

"How about in the middle?"

The lights in the theater were starting to go down and latecomers were starting to grab the few remaining seats. "Fine."

They hurried to their seats and Will placed the container of popcorn between their seats. As soon as the movie started, Jennifer closed her eyes. Every horror movie started with a murder and this one was no exception.

"Tell me when it's over," Jennifer whispered.

"Okay."

Jennifer listened to the creepy music build. Then she heard a scream.

"It's over," Will said.

Jennifer opened her eyes just as a guy wearing a clown mask jumped out from behind a bedroom door, lunging with a chain saw. The girl in the bedroom started to scream as the screen turned blood-red and the opening credits began.

Jennifer shrieked in fright and smacked Will on the arm. "You creep! You lied to me!"

Will was laughing hysterically, clutching his stomach. "You should have seen the way you jumped out of your seat! You jumped so high, I thought your head was going to hit the ceiling!"

"That wasn't very nice," Jennifer grumbled.

Will snickered. "No, but you have to admit it was funny."

Jennifer watched most of the movie through squinted eyes. Sometimes she looked away from the screen. More than once, she gripped Will's arm, burying her face in his shoulder. Finally, the movie ended. But not before the usual twist ending where the supposedly dead killer came back to life so everyone in the movie theater could jump out of their seats one last time.

"That was awful!" Jennifer exclaimed as they walked out of the theater.

Will stared at his shirt sleeve. "You were really scared. I think you almost shredded my shirt."

"I told you I didn't like horror movies!"

"Next time we'll see what you want."

"There's going to be a next time?" Jennifer asked, wondering what Will meant by his comment.

"I owe you for that trick I pulled when the movie started."

Jennifer tried not to feel let down. What was she expecting? For Will to fall for her and want to take her on a *real* date? Not that she was interested in him as boyfriend material. This wasn't one of those romantic comedies where the bickering main characters wound up together by the end of the movie.

"I have that list you asked for," Will said, reaching into the inside pocket of his motorcycle jacket. "Want to go over it together?"

"Sure."

"I don't know about you, but I'm kind of hungry."

"Me too."

"Let's grab a bite at The Burger Hut."

Jennifer knew that The Burger Hut was where everyone went after their Friday-night dates. This wasn't a date, but it couldn't hurt to be seen there together. Of course, they were going to be surrounded by real couples, which would only remind her that she didn't have a boyfriend.

Suddenly, Jennifer was no longer hungry.

"Are you going to give me the silent treatment the entire night?" Tom asked Natalie as they walked out of the movie theater.

"Why not? Don't you think you deserve it?"

"I said I was sorry for what happened last night."

Natalie thought back to the night before. When she'd gotten home, she'd told Tom their study date was off. Then she'd avoided him all day at school. When he showed up that night to take her on their date, she had walked out to his car without a word. He had tried making chitchat during the drive — he'd even tuned the radio to her favorite station — but she hadn't answered him. Only when they got to the movie theater did he apologize for his behavior the night before. Natalie hadn't said anything. She'd just taken her ticket from Tom and found herself a seat.

"You said it but I don't believe you meant it," Natalie said as they walked to Tom's car. "I still can't understand why you were so horrible to Leo."

"I was jealous," he admitted as he unlocked the car doors.

"Jealous?"

"What? I can't be jealous?" he asked as they got into the car and he turned on the heat. "I hate the idea of you being alone with another guy."

Natalie stared at Tom in disbelief. "Did you think I was going to cheat on you?"

"No! But I'm sure Leo was getting ideas. You're a knockout, Nat. I'm sure he's never spent so much time alone with a pretty girl."

"Leo wasn't going to make a move on me!"

"You don't know that. I wanted to make sure he knew you were my girlfriend and not to mess with me."

Natalie rolled her eyes as she buckled her seat belt. "Spare me the caveman routine!"

Tom leaned across his seat and gave Natalie a kiss. "I'm sorry. I don't know what came over me last night. It'll never happen again," he promised. "Am I forgiven?"

His apology did seem more genuine this time. It didn't feel like he was just saying what she wanted to hear. "Forgiven."

"How about we go to The Burger Hut?" he asked as he pulled the car out into the street.

"Okay."

Natalie knew that she should be flattered over Tom's jealousy. Being jealous meant he had feelings for her, didn't it?

Wasn't that supposed to make her happy?

But she didn't feel happy.

No matter how hard she tried, she couldn't forget the look of hurt on Leo's face.

Because she could remember feeling that same hurt years ago.

The Burger Hut was packed. Jennifer and Will gave their names to the hostess, who told them there would be a twenty-minute wait. They had just sat down in the waiting area when Natalie Bauer and Tom Marland walked in.

"Uh-oh," Jennifer said, nervously chewing on her lower lip.

"What?" Will asked.

"Here come Natalie Bauer and Tom Marland."

"So?"

"Natalie is Claudia's best friend."

Will rubbed his hands together. "Test run! If we can fool her, we can fool the Evil One! Are you ready to be a couple?"

Jennifer gulped. "As ready as I'll ever be."

The first person Natalie saw when she walked into The Burger Hut was Jennifer Harris. And she wasn't alone. She was sitting with a guy who had his arms wrapped around her, whispering in her ear. Natalie took a closer look at him. She couldn't believe her eyes. It was Will Sinclair.

From the way it looked, Will was Jennifer's new boyfriend.

Natalie was glad to see Jennifer hadn't been lying and she really did have a boyfriend.

If she hadn't . . .

Natalie shuddered.

She hated to imagine what Claudia would have done.

"I'm going to give my name to the hostess," Tom said, unbuttoning his coat.

As Tom walked away, Natalie went over to Jennifer and Will. "Hey!" she said.

A startled Jennifer pulled away from Will. "Hi, Natalie."

"Been waiting long?"

"We just got here."

Tom came over to join them. "A booth just opened up. The hostess says she can seat us if we can find another two people to sit with us."

"Want to join us?" Natalie asked.

Before Jennifer could answer, Will cut in. "We'd love to!"

"Are you crazy?" Jennifer hissed under her breath as they followed after Natalie and Tom to their booth.

"What are you freaking out about? I thought you wanted to see if we could fool her."

"All we had to do was say hello and chitchat

for a little bit. Now we're going to be sitting across from them for at least an hour. Maybe longer!"

Will shrugged. "What can I say, Red? I like living dangerously. Life's no fun if you're always playing it safe."

"You're not going to have a life after tonight if we don't fool them. And for the last time, don't call me Red!"

Were they buying it? Jennifer wondered as she ate her cheeseburger. *Did they think she and Will were a couple?*

They were sitting opposite Natalie and Tom. Will had pulled her close to him and had his arm wrapped around her shoulders. Every so often he would casually move his hand down her arm, rubbing it softly. Other times he would offer her bites from his fork and sips from his milk shake.

Natalie hadn't asked them a lot of questions. They had compared notes on the movies they'd seen — Natalie and Tom had seen *Romancing Rachel* — and talked about their classes. Jennifer felt something was going on between Natalie and Tom. She couldn't figure out what it was, but she sensed that they were in the middle of a fight. There wasn't that warmth you usually saw between couples. They were icy and polite to each other.

"Who do you think is going to be voted Most Romantic Couple?" Tom asked after they had ordered dessert.

"If you ask Claudia, she thinks it's going to be her and Chase," Natalie said.

"Do you think they'll win?" Will asked.

Natalie shrugged. "I don't know."

"Claudia might find herself facing a little competition," Jennifer said.

"From who?" Tom asked.

"Us!" Jennifer snuggled up to Will. "Of course, we still have to wait and see if we get nominated."

"If I were you, I wouldn't underestimate the competition," Tom said. "A lot of couples submitted essays and most of them have been together a lot longer than you and Will. Claudia and Chase have been together since freshman year. You two just started dating."

"You and Natalie haven't been a couple very long, either," Will said.

"I didn't submit an essay," Natalie said. "It never even occurred to me. Maybe it's because subconsciously I knew Claudia wouldn't like us competing against her."

Jennifer noticed that Tom wanted to say something, but he didn't. Was he mad that Natalie hadn't submitted an essay because she was afraid of Claudia?

"Well, Claudia *is* going to have some competition if she and Chase get nominated," Jennifer said. "They're going to be up against four other couples. I guess we're just going to have to wait until Monday to see who gets nominated and then let the voting begin."

Chapter Nine

Jennifer hated working on Saturday mornings.

The last place she wanted to be was at DeVille's. She'd rather be home in her pj's in front of the TV, watching cartoons and eating a nice sugary bowl of cereal the way she used to when she was younger. Instead, she was standing behind a cash register at the crack of 10 A.M.

Jennifer yawned as she stared around her empty department. She hated working in Bridal. The customers were *so* demanding. When she'd first been assigned to the department, she'd been thrilled, thinking she'd be working with happy brides-to-be. Wrong! Most of the women she dealt with were spoiled, demanding, whiny, and just not nice! They seemed to think because they were going to be a BRIDE that they could do or say whatever they wanted. Jennifer got the whole "I want my wedding day to be perfect" thing, but these women were out of control. In her opinion, that TV show *Bridezillas* should come to DeVille's and hide a secret video camera. They'd have enough material for at least a year's worth of episodes.

Jennifer began flipping through a bridal magazine. Even though she had told Will she didn't want a wedding, she couldn't help but wonder what it would be like to wear one of these gowns.

Thinking of Will reminded her of the night before. After finishing at the diner, he had started walking her home when his cell phone rang. It was his mother, calling in a panic because his father was out of town and one of the pipes in their basement had burst. Water was gushing everywhere and she didn't know what to do. Will promised to get home right away. When he got off the phone, Jennifer told him she could walk home by herself.

"Are you sure?" he had asked.

"Go," she had insisted. "Your mom needs you. We'll talk tomorrow."

After he left, Jennifer wondered what would have happened if Will had walked her home.

Would he have given her a kiss good night? She hadn't been expecting a full-on-the-lips-end-of-a-date kind of kiss. But maybe a quick peck on the cheek?

The bell in front of Jennifer's cash register clanged, startling her from her thoughts. She looked up from the magazine and saw she had a customer.

It was Claudia. What was she doing in the bridal department?

"We'd like some service here!" Claudia snapped. "I'm sure DeVille's isn't paying you to read magazines!"

Jennifer closed the magazine and gave Claudia her most professional smile. "How can I help you?"

Claudia pointed to a young woman flipping through a book of wedding invitations. "That's my sister Pam. She's getting married in October."

Jennifer walked out from behind the register, bringing along one of the folders they used for registering new brides. "Good morning," she said. "See anything you like?"

Pam curled her lip in a way that was similar to Claudia's. The two could have been identical twins, they looked so much alike. The only difference between them was the huge engagement ring on Pam's finger.

"Are you in charge?" Pam asked.

"No, I'm not."

"Where's your boss?"

"Mrs. Hudson won't be in until twelve o'clock."

Pam slammed shut the invitation book. "I don't do assistants."

"Pam doesn't do assistants," Claudia repeated.

Jennifer kept a smile on her face, reminding herself that the customer was always right. "While Mrs. Hudson has more experience than me, perhaps I can show you a few things, and if you have any questions, she can answer them."

Pam checked the time on her watch. Jennifer couldn't help but notice it was gold and decorated with diamonds. "As long as we're here, we might as well," Pam huffed, plopping herself down on a couch. She snapped her fingers. "Show us some wedding gowns."

"And make it fast!" Claudia added with a snap of her own as she sat next to her sister.

Jennifer went into the back and found the most expensive wedding gowns they had. She had a feeling Pam wasn't going to want to see anything cheap. When she brought the gowns out, she displayed them one at a time, explaining all the special touches. Each time she finished her explanation, Pam and Claudia would make a face. They kept doing the same thing until Jennifer ran out of wedding gowns.

"These all look cheap and tacky," Pam said. "Doesn't DeVille's carry any designer gowns?"

Jennifer peeked at the price tags of the gowns she had brought out. Most of them were at least a thousand dollars. How much more expensive did she want?

Pam turned to Claudia. "We should have gone to Vera Wang."

Vera Wang! Jennifer knew those wedding gowns cost thousands and thousands of dollars. Spending that much on a dress you were only going to wear for one day was crazy!

"What kind of fabric do you have for bridesmaid gowns?" Pam asked.

After returning the wedding gowns to the back, Jennifer brought out a fabric book filled with all sorts of colors. Pam quickly flipped through the cloth pages, vetoing all of Jennifer's suggestions.

"My bridesmaids can't look prettier than me," Pam said. "We need to find a color that's going to make them look washed out."

"With the exception of me, of course," Claudia added.

"Claudia is going to be my maid of honor," Pam told Jennifer. "So her dress will be different from theirs."

"How about pea green?" Claudia suggested.

"I was thinking more of a watery lemon."

"We could have them wear black!" Claudia exclaimed.

"Are you getting married on Halloween?" Jennifer asked.

"No," Pam said. "October twenty-fourth. Why?"

Jennifer shrugged. "Just wondering. Halloween is on a Saturday this year and we've had lots of brides with that date come in." *Plus, it seems like the perfect date for a witch like you.*

Pam got off the couch. "Let's go, Claudia. I don't know why Mother insisted we come here. It's obvious I'm going to need to do all this in Manhattan."

Without even a thank you for all her help, Pam walked away from Jennifer.

"Still coming to my party tonight?" Claudia asked before following after her sister.

"I wouldn't miss it."

"And you're bringing your boyfriend, right?"

Jennifer could see the way Claudia was studying her. Like she was waiting to hear some sort of excuse. "Who else would I bring?"

"I can't wait to meet him."

"He's dying to meet you, too."

"Really?"

"I've told him all about you." *Every nasty, horrible thing you've ever done.*

"Pam's going to buy me a new outfit for my party." Claudia pointed to a mannequin across the aisle in the designer dress department. "That one. She works in PR in New York, so she knows what's hot and what's not."

"I'm getting a new outfit, too."

"Is Old Navy having a sale?" Claudia snickered.

Jennifer could feel her temper rising. She hated the way Claudia was always putting her down. Just once, she'd like to leave her speechless. Before she could stop herself, Jennifer pointed to another mannequin in the designer dress department. "That's the outfit I'm buying."

Claudia walked over to the mannequin and checked the price tag on the dress. "Expensive."

Jennifer joined Claudia and peeked at the price. She gulped. The dress was five hundred dollars! She didn't have that kind of money. Even with her store discount, she still couldn't afford the dress.

Claudia stared closely at Jennifer. "What's the matter, Jen? You've suddenly gone pale."

Jennifer pointed up at the ceiling. "It's the fluorescent lighting. It washes you out."

"Uh-huh. Sure it's not the price of the dress? It's five hundred dollars. Not fifty. There's an extra zero."

"I can afford it," Jennifer confidently said, even though she didn't feel it.

"How fab! I can't wait to see you in it." Claudia found her dress on a rack and headed over to the cash register. "Bye!"

Jennifer watched Claudia and Pam pay for the dress. As soon as they stepped into an elevator and were gone, Jennifer whipped out her cell phone and called Violet.

"Come on! Answer!" she pleaded with the ringing phone.

Finally, she heard a click, followed by, "Mmghgramhh."

"Violet, wake up. Wake up!"

"Huh? What?" a sleepy voice asked. "Who is it?"

"Jennifer! I need your help."

"What's up?"

"I did it again."

"Did what?"

"Opened my big mouth and lied."

Violet sighed. "Let me guess. Claudia?"

"Who else?"

"What happened this time?"

Jennifer told Violet the entire story. "What am I going to do? I can't afford five hundred dollars."

Violet yawned. "Here's an easy solution. Wear something else."

"I can't! She thinks I'm not going to show up in that dress and I have to!"

"Okay, calm down. Let me think about this."

There was silence on the other end of the line.

"Are you still there?" a panicked Jennifer asked.

"Yes! Give me a minute. I just woke up. And you cheated me out of a great dream. I was on a date with the Jonas Brothers and they were all fighting over me!"

"Sorry."

"You *so* owe me!" Violet was quiet for a couple of minutes. Then she said, "I have an idea. But it's risky."

"What? What? I'll do anything."

"You still have that emergency credit card your parents gave you, right?"

"Yes."

"Charge the dress on the card but don't take off the tags. You wear the dress tonight and then return it tomorrow. No one will be the wiser. Especially if you snatch the credit card bill before your parents see it!"

Jennifer's body sagged with relief. "Violet, you're a genius! Why didn't I think of that?"

"Because you're not a genius. Now if you don't mind, I want to go back to sleep. I'll talk to you later."

After getting off the phone with Violet, Jennifer found the dress in her size and hurried to the nearest cash register. She needed to get back to her own register before someone noticed she was gone. As she did, she stopped in her tracks and groaned.

Could her day get any worse?

Mindy Yee was walking her way.

Jennifer looked for a dressing room to duck into, but they were all taken.

"Jennifer!" Mindy called out when she spotted her.

There was no avoiding it. "Mindy!" Jennifer exclaimed with a smile. "Hi!"

"Girl, we need to talk!"

"About what?"

Mindy playfully swatted Jennifer on the arm. "Don't pretend with me! You know what! You have to tell me all about this Mystery Guy of yours!"

"If I told you, he wouldn't be a mystery anymore, now would he?"

"So he *does* exist? Rumor has it that you made him up."

I can just imagine who told you that rumor, Jennifer thought. *And I'm sure you're the one who's been spreading it, since you're the biggest gossip at North Ridge High.*

"He exists," Jennifer said. "Natalie Bauer got to meet him last night."

"She did?"

"Yes, but I swore her to secrecy."

Luckily, Natalie had agreed not to let the cat out of the bag. And although The Burger Hut had been packed, there hadn't been anyone else she'd recognized from school. Claudia was still in the dark and she planned on keeping it that way until tonight.

"So you're bringing him to Claudia's party?"

"Yes. You can meet him there."

"Can't wait!"

Jennifer decided to deflect Mindy's attention off her. She pointed to the stack of clothes tossed over Mindy's arm. If there was one thing Mindy loved talking about, it was herself. "Doing a little shopping?"

"I'm celebrating!" Mindy exclaimed. "My father's restaurants are going national! You know, like McDonald's or Burger King!"

Jennifer knew Mindy's father owned a chain of upscale Chinese restaurants called House of Yee. They made the best egg rolls in town.

"That's great."

"I told Daddy we're going to need a catchphrase, and we should say our food is *Yeelicious.* What do you think?"

Yeeucky! Jennifer thought.

"There might even be commercials!" Mindy added. "Can you imagine me on TV?"

Jennifer wished Mindy was on TV right now. She'd aim the remote control at her and turn her off.

"I'd love to chat some more, but I've got to pay for this dress and get back to my department,"

Jennifer said, walking around Mindy to the cash register and placing the dress on the counter.

Mindy peeked at Jennifer's dress. "I love it! I've got the same one in three different colors. Don't you love shopping here?"

If I could afford it, I would, Jennifer thought, trying not to cringe as the cashier rang up her dress and swiped her credit card.

Natalie's neighborhood video store always had the best DVDs. They had a wide variety of films and she always managed to find something to take home. Usually, she rented old black-and-white romantic comedies because she loved the witty dialogue and screwball antics. Today she had found six movies she wanted to see, including *It Happened One Night*, which was from the 1930s.

Natalie wished Tom felt the same way about the movies she liked, but he didn't. He liked watching movies that had car chases and tons of explosions. Days after seeing one of those movies, Natalie never remembered anything about the plot. It was usually all a blur. There was never any sort of character development or smart dialogue. It was just another thing that they didn't have in common. The only reason he'd agreed to see *Romancing Rachel* last night was that he was trying to make up with her. She'd seen him peeking at his watch more than once during the movie.

When Natalie brought her DVDs to the front of the store, she was surprised to see Leo standing behind the counter.

"Leo!" she exclaimed. "What are you doing here?"

Leo looked just as surprised to see her. "I work here."

"Since when?"

"I started a week ago." He reached for the DVD cases Natalie was holding and started swiping the backs of them with a silver wand. "You're renting a lot of movies."

"We're supposed to be getting a big snowstorm this weekend. I figured I'd stock up in case we get snowbound."

There was an awkward moment of silence after that. It was the first time Natalie was seeing Leo since Thursday night. What happened that night remained unspoken between them. Did she say something? Apologize for Tom's behavior? She couldn't pretend it hadn't happened.

"About the other night," Natalie began.

Leo waved a hand at her. "You don't have to say anything."

"But I feel like I do."

"Why? It wasn't your fault. Besides, I'm used to it."

Hearing those words, Natalie found herself getting angry. "You shouldn't have to be used to it."

"Hey, that's life in high school. There's a pecking order and I'm on the bottom. You're at the top. So is Tom."

"Don't say that! You make it sound like I'm something special when I'm not."

"Are you serious?" Leo asked in disbelief, his own anger showing. "Have you looked in a mirror? You're gorgeous. Not only that, but you're best friends with two of the most popular girls at North Ridge High and you're dating one of our star athletes. If this was a game of poker, you'd have the winning hand."

"And that's why you think I'm better than everyone else?" Natalie asked. "I'm not! I'm just like you."

Leo laughed bitterly. "No, you're not."

"You don't know anything about me!" Natalie exploded, hating the way Leo was prejudging her.

"That's true," Leo conceded. "I will say that you're not like the rest of them. You're nice."

"Thanks," she said, feeling less angry although she really had no reason to *be* angry. Leo was the one who had been wronged.

Leo handed Natalie her DVDs. "All set. I see you've checked out *Breakfast at Tiffany's*."

"I've seen it around ten times. I love Audrey Hepburn movies."

"Have you seen *Sabrina*?"

"Of course!"

"*Roman Holiday*?"

"Yes."

"Okay, I'm going to stump you. *Wait Until Dark*?"

Natalie shook her head. "I've never heard of that one."

"She made it in the late 1960s. It's a suspense movie. She plays a blind woman who's being stalked. It's got some scary moments."

"What kind of movies do you like to watch?"

"I'll watch anything," Leo said. "Right now I'm into foreign films and Japanese horror."

"Weren't a couple of those Japanese horror movies remade in English?"

"There have been a couple. *The Ring*, *The Grudge*, and *Dark Water* are the three biggest."

"I saw all of those. They were creepy."

"The Japanese versions are creepier. We should have a movie marathon one night and watch both versions."

"That would be fun."

"Doing anything tonight?"

Natalie was caught off guard by Leo's invitation and it took her a second to answer. "I wish I could, but I've got plans."

Leo busied himself with checking in DVDs that had been returned. "Bummer. Maybe another time. Guess I'll see you around."

Natalie could tell Leo didn't believe her. *He probably thinks I turned him down because he's fat.*

Natalie wondered how hard it had been for Leo to ask her to hang out with him.

"I just had an idea," Natalie said. "If you're not doing anything tonight, maybe you want to come to the party I'm going to."

Leo tore his eyes away from the DVDs in his hands. "Where is it?"

"My friend Claudia's house."

"Claudia Monroe?"

"Yes."

An expression of sheer terror washed over Leo's face. "I think I'll pass."

"Why?"

"I don't think Monster Monroe would like me being there. Besides, she didn't invite me."

Natalie waved a hand. "That doesn't matter. Claudia's parties are always huge. Lots of people crash. And *I'm* inviting you."

"I don't know. . . ." Leo reluctantly said.

"Think about it," Natalie urged.

"I'll think about it," Leo agreed. "If I decide to go, you'll see me there."

"I'll be looking for you," Natalie said as she walked out of the store.

And she would.

It would be nice to see a friendly face at the party.

Chapter Ten

"Wow!" Violet exclaimed as she walked into Jennifer's bedroom. "You look fantastic!"

Jennifer pressed a finger to her lips. "Shhhh!" she warned. "I don't want my parents to hear you."

Violet unzipped her parka and flopped down on Jennifer's bed. A snoozing Sheba, who was nestled on Jennifer's pillow, opened one eye, stared at Violet, and then went back to sleep. "They're all the way downstairs. Why are you being so paranoid?"

Jennifer closed her bedroom door. "So far neither my mom or my dad has seen me in this dress and I plan to keep it that way. They're getting ready to leave for their weekly bridge game, so I should be safe. If they were to see it, I'm sure one of them would ask me a zillion questions and I don't want to lie to them."

Violet held up two fingers and pressed them together. "You'd only be telling a little white lie."

"Lying is lying."

"But you're lying to Claudia," Violet pointed out.

"That's different."

"How?"

"I'm not really *lying* to Claudia," Jennifer explained as she put on her gold hoop earrings. "I'm playing a joke on her."

Violet adjusted her cat-eye glasses and stared at Jennifer. "Uh-huh."

"And Claudia's not going to ground me if she finds out the truth!"

"Nooooo," Violet slowly said. "But she'll do a lot worse!"

"Maybe she will," Jennifer admitted. "But I'd rather take my chances with her than with my folks! If Will and I can fool her for a little bit, it will be worth it. Think of all the times she's been mean and horrible to so many people at school. And she never paid Will for those pizzas!"

"Is Will picking you up?" Violet asked, reaching for the copy of *Seventeen* that was on Jennifer's nightstand and flipping through it.

Jennifer checked the time on her clock radio. "He should be getting here any minute."

"Jennifer! We're leaving!" her father called from the first floor.

Jennifer stuck her head out her bedroom door. "Have a good time!"

"You too," her mother said.

"Don't forget your curfew," her father added.

"Don't worry, I'll be home by twelve thirty," she promised.

After closing the bedroom door, Jennifer turned to the mirror over her dresser and examined herself one last time. The dress was plum-colored and tied around her neck like a halter top. She was wearing high-heeled black slouchy boots with it. She'd used hot rollers so her hair was a wild mane of loose curls, and applied smoky plum eye shadow to her lids and some blush to her cheeks. In addition to the gold hoop earrings, the only other jewelry she was wearing was a bunch of bangle bracelets on one arm.

"Do you think Will will like what I'm wearing?"

Violet's eyes widened in panic behind her glasses and she dropped the copy of *Seventeen*. "Why do you care what Will thinks?"

Jennifer shrugged. "I don't know. I guess my mind is automatically in date mode."

"Well, get it *out* of date mode. Remember, this is not a *real* date. Will is *not* your boyfriend. This is all fake, remember?"

"Yes, yes, I remember," she said as she gave herself a spritz of perfume.

Violet sternly pointed a finger at Jennifer. "Good. *Don't* forget it!"

The doorbell rang and Jennifer turned to Violet. "He's here!"

"Talk about timing. He just missed your parents."

Jennifer took one last look in her mirror before leaving the bedroom with Violet right behind her.

"Why do I feel like an actress about to go on stage?" Jennifer asked as they hurried down the stairs.

"Relax," Violet said. "You told me the two of you fooled Natalie and Tom last night."

"That's different. Natalie isn't suspicious of me."

"Just do whatever you did last night."

"Good advice," Jennifer said as she opened the front door.

"Ready to enter Claudia's evil lair?" Will asked as he stepped inside.

"As ready as I'll ever be," Jennifer said as she reached into the hall closet for her coat. She could feel Will's eyes studying her from behind.

"Like what you see?" she asked, turning around with a saucy smile.

Will was silent for a moment. Then he said, "I'm definitely surprised. Who knew you could look so hot?"

Will's words left Jennifer speechless. He thought she looked *hot*? That wasn't what she'd been expecting to hear. But she'd take it!

"You might have to beat the guys off at this party," Will said.

"Don't you mean *you're* going to have to beat them off?" Jennifer reminded him as she pulled on her gloves. "After all, you're my boyfriend."

"*Fake* boyfriend," Violet piped up as her eyes worriedly flickered back and forth between Jennifer and Will.

"I'm not the jealous type," Will told Jennifer. "But don't worry. I'll be keeping my eyes on you the entire night. I wouldn't want you trading me in for some other guy."

"Shouldn't *I* be the one worried about getting traded in?" Jennifer asked. "After all, you're the one who always has a new girlfriend."

"I don't think either one of you has anything to worry about since this is all *pretend*," Violet reminded them.

"Are you coming to this party?" Will asked.

Violet laughed. "Claudia would *never* invite me to one of her parties. She's been snubbing me since third grade. I'm going home." Violet gave Jennifer a hug good night. "I'll talk to you tomorrow. Good luck!"

Violet left, with Will following after her, leaving Jennifer to turn off the hall lights and lock the front door. When she got outside, she saw Will leaning against the side of a red car parked at the curb.

"No motorcycle?" she asked.

"I borrowed my older sister's car. I figured it was too cold for the motorcycle. Disappointed?"

"Well, I was wondering what it would be like to sit behind you with my arms wrapped around you and the wind blowing through my hair," Jennifer admitted.

"I'll give you a ride another day."

"Promise?"

Will crossed his heart. "Promise." He studied Jennifer from head to toe. "I never saw you as a biker chick."

"There's a lot you don't know about me, Mr. Sinclair," she said as she got into the front seat.

"Guess I better start finding out," Will said as he went around to the driver's side and opened the door. "Because it's almost showtime!"

Will and Jennifer tossed questions back and forth to each other on the drive to Claudia's house. They knew their answers but both were aware there was more to their charade than just knowing the right answers.

"Leave most of the talking to me," Jennifer said. "Girls are always gushing about their boyfriends. Guys usually don't like to talk."

"True," Will agreed.

"A lot of it is going to be body language. Holding. Touching. Like last night."

"Piece of cake," Will said. "We did a pretty good job fooling Natalie and Tom."

Jennifer knew last night had gone well. But like she told Violet, Natalie wasn't Claudia. They were going to have to be on their guard the entire night. They couldn't afford any slipups.

When they arrived at Claudia's house, a line of cars was parked in the driveway, as well as double-parked in the street.

"Looks like there's already a huge crowd," Will said as he parked behind the last car in the driveway. He took Jennifer's hand in his. "Ready?"

Jennifer squeezed his hand, fighting against the butterflies in her stomach. "As ready as I'll ever be."

"We can do this," Will said. "We can."

Jennifer didn't say anything. She just nodded, wishing she had Will's confidence.

Claudia's entire house was lit up. It was a huge McMansion with three floors. As they approached the front door, they could hear music blasting.

"I don't believe it," Jennifer said as they walked inside.

The house was decorated for Valentine's Day.

There were tons of red, white, and pink balloons floating in the air. Pink and red streamers were draped around the staircase leading to the second floor and foiled hearts and cupids were pinned on the walls. But what got the most attention — and shocked Jennifer — was the huge pink banner strung across the living room that said VOTE FOR CLAUDIA AND CHASE! The flat-screen TV in the family room showed nonstop clips of Claudia and Chase, dating all the way back to freshman year, and there were poster-size photos of Claudia and Chase hanging from the ceiling of every room with invisible wire.

They had walked into a shrine devoted to Claudia and Chase.

"I feel like we're in enemy territory," Will whispered.

"Me too," Jennifer whispered back as she stared into a bowl of candy hearts. She picked one up and saw it said CLAUDIA LOVES CHASE. Another said: C + C 4EVER.

"Talk about confidence," Will said. "I guess she figures her nomination is in the bag."

Jennifer dropped the candy heart back into the bowl. "There's a difference between being nominated and winning."

Will looked around the party. "So where is the Evil One?"

"Good question," Jennifer said, wondering exactly the same thing.

"Where's Claudia?" Eden asked Natalie.

"I think she's up in her bedroom. Why?"

Eden didn't wait for an answer. She was too angry. Instead, she stormed up the stairs to the third floor. When she got to Claudia's bedroom, she didn't bother to knock and barged right in.

A startled Claudia looked away from the mirror at her vanity table, where she was sitting and applying her lipstick.

"Did you forget how to knock?"

"How could you do this to me?" Eden wailed.

Claudia capped her lipstick and picked up a hairbrush. "Do what?"

"Invite Keith to your party! He's here. With his new girlfriend!"

"What was I supposed to do?" Claudia asked as she started brushing her hair. "Not invite him?"

"Yes!"

"How could I? He's one of Chase's best friends."

"And you're supposed to be *my* best friend." Eden hadn't really wanted to come to Claudia's party, but Claudia had given her a massive guilt trip when she'd called that afternoon. Finally, she had caved in and said she would come. "You could have warned me so I wouldn't have been blindsided when I walked through the front door and found them in the living room. Do you know what it was like for me to see Deena sitting on Keith's lap?"

Claudia put down her hairbrush. "It slipped my mind."

I'll just bet it did, Eden thought darkly. She knew how much Claudia loved causing drama.

Sometimes Eden asked herself why she was still friends with Claudia. True, there were times when Claudia could be kind and thoughtful. Often she would invite her to spend long weekends with her family at their house in the Hamptons during the summer, or at their ski lodge in upstate New York during the winter. She was always giving her clothes she didn't want anymore — some with the price tags still on them. Their friendship went back to junior high, when they had found themselves with identical schedules. Because they were in the same classes, they often ended up talking between periods or during lunch. As they got to know each other, they started hanging out after school and soon they were making weekend plans together. It continued when they started high school and Natalie became friends with them.

But over the last year, Claudia had started to change. She'd always been a bit mean . . . but never to Eden and Natalie. But more and more, Claudia was showing her nasty side to them and Eden didn't like it. Neither she nor Natalie deserved to be treated this way. Not when they were supposed to be Claudia's best friends.

"What am I supposed to do?" Eden asked.

"Ignore them!" Claudia exclaimed, walking to her bedroom door. "Have a good time. This is a huge house. I'm sure you can find someplace to hide from them, although if I were you, I'd find a hot guy to dance with and show Keith that you've moved on!"

After Claudia left, Eden went over to the vanity table and checked her appearance in the mirror. At least she had pulled out all the stops with her outfit. It didn't look like she was nursing a broken heart. She was wearing a strapless white silk ruffle top and a short chocolate-brown suede skirt with matching boots. To bring more attention to her dangling chandelier earrings, she had pulled her hair back into a slick ponytail. She looked pretty and confident. She only wished she felt that way.

She wanted to go home, but she couldn't leave. Not yet. If she did, Deena and Keith would think they'd scared her off, and she wasn't going to let them think that! So she went down to the kitchen and decided to get a soda. She'd stay for an hour and then leave.

But when Eden entered the kitchen, she found another nasty surprise.

Leaning against the kitchen counter, having salsa and chips fed to him by a tall cocoa-skinned girl with blonde dreadlocks, was her ex-boyfriend Luther. After the girl would pop a chip into his mouth, Luther would give her a kiss. She'd then kiss him back before popping another chip into his mouth.

It was obvious to Eden that they were boyfriend and girlfriend. She could tell by the way they were acting.

Eden ducked out of the kitchen before being

seen. She didn't want to talk to Luther and meet his new girlfriend. Like Keith, Luther had never given her a reason when he'd broken up with her last summer. He'd said, "I'm just not feeling it anymore."

At least he'd done it in person and not by text message.

Now that the kitchen and living room were off-limits, where else could she go?

She decided on the rec room. It should be safe down there.

Eden headed down to the basement, and as she got closer, she could hear music blaring. It was an old Madonna song from the 80s. At the sound of the music, Eden found herself swaying. She loved to dance.

As she grooved to the music, Eden noticed a couple dancing together in a corner. Even though it wasn't a slow dance, they had their arms wrapped around each other's necks. But they were more focused on kissing than dancing. As they stepped out of the shadows into the light, Eden's eyes widened in shock.

The guy holding the girl was Malcolm, another one of her ex-boyfriends.

Had Claudia invited *all* her exes?

Eden no longer wanted to dance. Before Malcolm could see her, she left the rec room and went back upstairs, where she found her coat buried under a pile in the front hallway.

"Where are you going?" Natalie asked as she passed by her.

"Home!" Eden exclaimed.

Before going home, Eden stopped at the supermarket. If she was going to feel sorry for herself, she needed to do it with some ice cream. She grabbed a small basket and headed for the ice cream aisle. After finding containers of Ben & Jerry's Chocolate Fudge Brownie and Mint Chocolate Chunk, she decided she needed a can of whipped cream.

She was walking down the dairy aisle when she saw the last person she expected to see on a Saturday night.

Dexter.

And he was with a pretty girl!

For Eden, it was the last straw. *Everyone* she knew was paired off. Even a brainiac like Dexter!

Was she the only person who was all alone on a Saturday night?

Before Eden could stop herself, tears were falling down her cheeks.

It was at that exact moment that Dexter turned around.

"Eden?" he asked in shock.

Eden quickly wiped away her tears, embarrassed to have been caught crying.

"Is everything okay?" he asked, coming over.

"Everything's fine!" she exclaimed, trying to smile.

"What are you doing here? I thought you'd be at Claudia's party."

At the mention of Claudia's party, Eden remembered why she had left and the tears returned. And this time, there was no holding them back.

"Everything's not fine," she sobbed. "I've had the worst night of my life. I ran into three of my ex-boyfriends and they all have new girlfriends."

"That must have been tough," Dexter said, his voice filled with sympathy.

"Why didn't they want me, Dexter? Am I that horrible?"

"Of course not!" Dexter quickly answered.

The pretty girl came over. She had shoulder-length brown corkscrew curls. "Is everything okay, Dex?"

Eden sniffed. "I'm sorry. I'm ruining your date."

Dexter laughed. "Date? What date? This is my sister Angie. She's a freshman at North Ridge High."

"Hi," Angie said, reaching into her purse for a tissue and handing it to Eden.

"Thanks," Eden said, blowing her nose.

"Why don't you come back to our house?" Angie suggested. "We were going to watch some movies. It might help you get your mind off things."

"I'm sure Eden wouldn't want to come over," Dexter hurriedly said. "She probably has other plans."

"I'd love to!" Eden exclaimed.

She didn't know why she had said yes. Maybe it was because Angie was so friendly. Or maybe it was because anything was better than being home alone.

Dexter's other two sisters were waiting when they got back from the supermarket. As soon as Dexter and Angie walked through the door, they were pulling at their bags.

"Did you get me potato chips?" one asked.

"Where are my pretzels?" the other demanded.

Dexter held the grocery bags over his head. "I got everything you wanted, but first I want you to say hello to a friend of mine. Eden, these are my other two sisters, Thelma and Yvonne."

"Hi," Eden said.

Twelve-year-old Thelma, who Eden thought resembled the singer Rihanna, said hi, but eight-year-old Yvonne hid behind Dexter, shyly peeking out at Eden. She was an adorable little girl with a head full of thick twisty braids held with colorful barrettes.

"I'm going to make hot chocolate," Angie said, heading into the kitchen. "Why don't you guys pick a movie?"

"What should we watch?" Thelma asked as they walked into the living room.

"*Dreamgirls*," Yvonne begged. "Please, please, please."

Dexter groaned. "We've already seen that five times."

"I don't mind seeing it again," Eden said as they sat down on a brown couch. She gazed around the living room. It was a warm, cozy room with a wood-burning fireplace, pumpkin-colored walls, and comfortable armchairs.

"Who's your favorite Dreamgirl?" Thelma asked, sitting next to Eden. Yvonne, meanwhile, stayed close to Dexter's side.

"I like Effie."

"Deena's my favorite."

Everyone loves Deena, Eden grumpily thought. *On-screen and off.*

"Why do you look so sad?" Thelma asked as Dexter turned the TV on and started to fiddle with the DVD player.

"My love life is a mess," Eden confessed.

"Were you crying?"

"A little bit," Eden confessed. Then she gave Thelma and Yvonne a smile. "But I'm feeling much better now."

"Yvonne," Angie called out from the kitchen, "come and help me."

"Are your folks out for the night?" Eden asked Dexter as Yvonne raced into the kitchen.

"They had a charity benefit to go to in Manhattan."

"So you're in charge?"

"Ha!" Angie laughed as she came into the living room carrying a tray filled with mugs of hot chocolate and putting it down on the coffee table. "That's what he likes to think. But we're the ones calling the shots."

Yvonne held a mug of hot chocolate out to Eden. "I put extra marshmallows in yours," she quietly said.

"You did?"

Yvonne nodded. "Extra marshmallows always make me feel better. Maybe they'll make you feel better, too."

Hearing those sweet words made Eden want to wrap her arms around Yvonne. "Thanks."

"I like your earrings," Yvonne said.

Eden flicked one with her finger. "Want to try them on?"

"Really?" Yvonne gasped.

"Sure," Eden said, taking them off and fastening them in Yvonne's pierced earlobes.

"How do I look?" Yvonne asked, preening for Eden. The earrings were a bit too long for someone so small, but she looked cute.

"I think you might have to grow into them. Why don't you put them away in your jewelry box? Then when you get older, you can wear them."

"You mean I can have them?" Yvonne gasped in disbelief.

you can have them. But
;hare them with Thelma,"
; there to be hurt feelings.
.e quickly replied.
that," Dexter said.
:ed, taking a sip of her hot
ys get another pair at the
)er expensive."
)f you." Dexter turned to
do you say, Yvonne?"
iile. "Thank you."
vie?" Dexter asked, turn-
and aiming the remote

ou?" Yvonne asked, snug-
the other side of the couch
nswer.
wrapping an arm around
better for the first time

Chapter Eleven

"So where is he?"

At the sound of Claudia's voice, Jennifer slowly turned around from the chocolate dessert bar. She had been trying to decide between a brownie and a mini éclair.

"Where's who?" Jennifer asked, deciding to play dumb.

"Your boyfriend."

"He's somewhere in this crowd."

Jennifer watched as Will walked across the living room. He was wearing a pair of Levi's, a blue denim shirt that was open at the collar, and a brown leather vest. He looked like a modern-day cowboy. All that was missing was a hat on his head.

"Here you go," Will said, handing Jennifer a glass of cranberry juice.

"What are you doing here?" Claudia asked. "I didn't invite you to my party."

"Yes, you did," Will answered.

Claudia shook her head. "No, I didn't."

"Okay, you didn't *personally* invite me," Will corrected her. "You told my girlfriend to bring me."

Claudia looked around. "And that's?"

"Me," Jennifer said as she toasted Claudia with her glass of cranberry juice and took a sip.

Jennifer wished she had a camera. Claudia's face went from confused to shocked to stunned in less than a minute as she stared back and forth between Jennifer and Will.

"The two of you are dating?" she asked when she found her voice.

"Since New Year's Eve," Jennifer said. "Don't you remember, Claudia? I told you at school. And then you were nice enough to invite me to your party and told me to bring Will."

"You've been dating for the last month?"

"Uh-huh," Will said.

"How come no one's seen the two of you out together?" Claudia suspiciously asked.

"We were taking things slow," Will said. "Not rushing into anything. We didn't want everyone gossiping about us so we spent a lot of time at each other's houses. Just hanging out. But we made it official this week. Lots of people saw us."

"Why this week? Why not last week or next week?"

Will wrapped an arm around Jennifer's waist, pulling her close. "I guess it's because Valentine's Day is coming. I want everyone to know she's mine. And then there's the Most Romantic Couple contest. We can't get votes if people don't know we're a couple."

"You have to get nominated first," Claudia icily replied.

"Shouldn't you be following your own advice?" Will asked, indicating all the VOTE FOR CLAUDIA AND CHASE signs.

Jennifer smothered a giggle. She thought Claudia's eyes were going to bug out of her head. *No one* ever dissed her that way. At least not to her face!

"We ran into Natalie and Tom last night after going to the movies," Jennifer said, wanting to distract Claudia's attention from Will. "We shared a booth with them at The Burger Hut."

Claudia stared at Jennifer. "Natalie didn't tell me that."

"I asked her to keep it a secret," Jennifer said without thinking.

As soon as the words were out of her mouth, Jennifer realized she had made a mistake.

"And she said she would?" Claudia hissed.

She didn't even wait for an answer as she angrily stormed off.

"Uh-oh," Jennifer said to Will. "I think I just messed up."

"Big time," Will agreed. "I would *not* want to be in Natalie's shoes when Claudia finds her."

Natalie was bored out of her mind.

She hadn't seen Tom since they'd arrived at the party. He'd disappeared with Chase and his other sports buddies to play with the Wii down in the basement. And Eden had left the party way too early. Something had upset her, but she'd run out so fast, Natalie hadn't had a chance to find out what was wrong.

Natalie sighed as she sipped the last of her Diet Coke from the red plastic cup she was holding. There were a bunch of familiar faces from school, but no one whom she considered a close friend. For some reason, that made her think of Leo. Even though she hardly knew him and was just learning more about him, she felt like she knew him better than most of the people here tonight. She wondered if he was going to take her up on her invitation and come to the party. Probably not.

She was walking back into the kitchen to refill her cup when Claudia grabbed her by the arm and pulled her into the bathroom.

"Hey! That hurts!" Natalie said as Claudia's long nails dug into her sleeve.

"How could you betray me this way?" Claudia demanded.

"Betray you?" Natalie was confused. "What are you talking about?"

"Jennifer and Will! Why didn't you tell me they were dating?"

That's what she was having a meltdown about? "Why? What's the big deal?"

"She caught me completely off guard! I looked like an idiot! I thought she'd drag along someone nerdy like Shermy Hansen, Violet's cousin, to pretend to be her boyfriend. I wasn't expecting her to show up with Will Sinclair! Do you know how high her stock is going to rise? Every girl at North Ridge High is going to want to know how she tamed the Heartbreaker!"

Was it her imagination or did Claudia seem a

little bit jealous? She vaguely remembered Claudia mentioning Will at one point over the summer. Something like if she were ever to cheat on Chase, she'd have to do it with a guy who was his complete opposite. Someone like Will Sinclair.

She could never ask Claudia if she was jealous of Jennifer. She'd do more than sink her nails into her arm. She'd tear it off!

"This guy has never had a girlfriend and suddenly he's dating Jennifer?" Claudia shook her head. "It doesn't make sense."

"Why not?" Natalie asked. "They seemed like they were into each other last night. Who can explain love? When it happens, it happens." Natalie waved her empty plastic cup. "If you're finished interrogating me, I'd like to get a refill."

"Don't ever keep a secret from me again, Nat," Claudia warned before stepping aside.

It was on the tip of Natalie's tongue to say, *Or what?* But she didn't. Instead, she went into the kitchen. As she was heading back to the living room, she could hear Claudia's voice. And it was nasty.

"What are you doing here, Blubber Boy? I didn't invite you. I think you took a wrong turn on the way to the all-you-can-eat buffet."

Natalie heard laughter.

"Now take your ginormous butt and get out! I'd have you thrown out but I don't think there are enough guys here to lift all that flab!"

There was more laughter.

When Natalie reached the living room and saw who everyone was laughing at, she almost dropped her red cup.

Leo!

She ran to his side. "Leo! You came!"

"And now I'm going," he said, heading for the front door.

"This fat loser thought he could crash my party," Claudia told Natalie.

"He's not crashing." Natalie placed a hand on Leo's arm so he would stay. "I invited him."

"*You* invited him?" Claudia asked in disbelief. "Why?"

"He's my friend."

"He's *your* friend," Claudia said. "Not my friend. And this is *my* party. Who said you could invite him? *No* fatties are allowed."

"This was a mistake," Leo said, shaking off Natalie's arm. "What was I thinking? I never should have come."

And then, before Natalie could stop him, before she could say she was sorry for the way he had been treated, Leo left the party.

★

e the way Claudia had
at was her problem?
Vill said.
n upset Natalie digging
s in the hallway. "I'll be

to Natalie's side. "Need

coat. It's a white parka
od is trimmed in fake

ng through the coats. "I
ter Leo, but don't. If you
audia madder."
t me."
et it slip that you knew

d out her wrinkled arm.
claws."

d my rabies shot," Natalie
d frantically searching
"*Where* is my coat?! I'm
e else's!"

"Natalie, don't leave," Jennifer repeated. "It's only going to make things worse. Plus, you also have a boyfriend. How would it look if you went running after another guy?"

Do I have a boyfriend? Natalie wondered. She hadn't seen Tom the entire night. He was too busy hanging out with his jock buddies. Talk about being ignored!

"If you leave, isn't Tom going to wonder where you are?"

That was true. With her luck, he'd come looking for her the second she left. And the last thing she wanted was another fight with him. She didn't think he'd be too happy if he heard she had gone running after Leo Barnes.

"Leo probably wants to be by himself right now," Jennifer pointed out. "I'll bet he's feeling embarrassed."

Natalie abandoned the coats and sat at the bottom of the staircase. "But this is all my fault," she said, feeling like crying. "I was the one who invited him to come tonight."

"It's not your fault," Jennifer said, sitting next to her. "And I'm sure Leo knows that. You didn't say all those horrible things to him. Claudia did. And you stuck up for him. I think you need to

ɔu can make things up

ː Jennifer's words and
ɪt."

them. "Want to dance?"

turned to Natalie. "Feel

ɪdia glaring at her across
vas mad. Madder than
lidn't think she'd be too
ith Jennifer and Will.

said, following Jennifer
:he basement while star-

: how much fun she was
's! She couldn't wait to

er. He knew how to move
weren't dancing, he was
ɪ wrapped around either
ːrs. Sometimes he would
ɪer ear. Other times he
nments about Claudia.

Everyone was coming up to her and Will, asking how long they'd been dating and wanting to know if they were going to compete as Most Romantic Couple. "We'll find out on Monday," Jennifer said whenever she was asked the question.

She was dancing to the latest hit from Fergie when someone bumped into her from behind. As she turned to see who it was, another person crashed into her from the side, spilling a glass of punch on the front of her dress.

"Ooops!" Claudia exclaimed. "Clumsy me!"

Jennifer stared at the growing stain in horror. No! No! No!

She ran from the basement up to the kitchen, searching for a napkin to dab at the stain.

"What's wrong?" Will asked, hurrying after her. "It's only a stain."

"You don't understand," Jennifer explained. "I don't own this dress."

"You borrowed it from a friend?"

"Sort of."

"What do you mean sort of?"

Making sure no one could hear her, Jennifer told Will of her plan to wear the dress and then return it.

"We've got to keep you away from Claudia," Will chuckled. "Who knows what that mouth of yours is going to make you do next."

"This isn't funny!" Jennifer exclaimed in panic. "I can't afford this dress. If it has a huge stain on it, I'm not going to be able to return it. That means I'll have to tell my parents what I did and they'll kill me for using my emergency credit card."

Will found a bottle of seltzer in the refrigerator. He poured some on a dish towel and Jennifer dabbed at the stain. "This should help for now. Let's go back to my house. My sister Maureen is really into vintage clothing. A lot of the old clothes she buys have stains on them but she's always able to get them out. She might be able to do something."

"You think?" Jennifer asked, trying not to get her hopes up.

"We'll never know unless she tries."

Maureen, who was a college sophomore, told Jennifer she'd be able to get the stain out. After lending Jennifer a pair of sweats and a T-shirt, she went to work on the dress, leaving Will and Jennifer in the living room.

"Want to watch a movie?" Will asked.

"You owe me a romantic comedy," Jennifer reminded him.

Will flicked through a stack of DVDs. "We don't have any of those, but how does *Mean Girls* sound?"

"After the night we just had? Perfect!"

After Will popped in the DVD, he shut off the lights and sat on the opposite end of the couch. Jennifer didn't know why, but she found herself wishing that Will were sitting closer to her. But why would he? Now that they were alone, they were no longer JENNIFERANDWILL, the couple. They were just Jennifer and Will.

By the time the movie was over, Maureen had returned with the dress.

"As good as new!" she proclaimed.

"The stain is gone," Jennifer marveled in amazement as she studied the front of the dress. "How'd you do it?"

"A little baking soda and a couple of other tricks I have up my sleeve."

After Jennifer changed back into the dress, Will offered to drive her home. They were both quiet during the drive. There was none of their usual bickering. When they reached her house, Will walked her to the front door.

"Looks like phase one of our plan was a success," he said.

Jennifer crossed her fingers. "So far. Now all we have to do is wait and see what happens on Monday."

Will stared at his cowboy boots. Then he looked up at Jennifer. "I had a lot of fun tonight."

A hank of Will's jet-black hair had fallen across his forehead. Jennifer was tempted to smooth it away. But she didn't. It seemed like something a real girlfriend would do. "Me too."

They stared at each other awkwardly.

Is he waiting for me to do something? Jennifer wondered. *Like kiss him?*

Before she could decide what to do, Will gave her a quick hug. Jennifer didn't even have a chance to wrap her arms around him before he pulled away. "I'll see you Monday at school. Unless you get a craving for pizza. I'll be delivering tomorrow."

Jennifer watched Will head back to his car and drive away.

The hug had been nice, but it wasn't what she'd been expecting.

She hated to admit it, but she'd been hoping for a good-night kiss.

Chapter Twelve

There was no school on Monday. It had started snowing heavily on Sunday afternoon and didn't stop until early Monday morning. When the storm was over, there was a foot of snow on the ground. As a result, all classes were canceled.

After lying in bed for an extra hour, Natalie got up and went down to the kitchen, where she found a note from her mother. Unfortunately, her parents hadn't gotten a snow day and were at work. Natalie's mother had left her a list of groceries to buy and also asked her to do the laundry.

Natalie munched on a slice of toasted raisin bread while watching morning TV. Then she cleaned up the kitchen, did two loads of laundry, folded and put everything away, and made her bed. The temperature was in the low teens so she bundled herself up in a black turtleneck, gray pullover sweater, black corduroy jeans, snow boots, and jacket. Then she wrapped a red knit scarf around her face and pulled her hood over her head before leaving the house.

With piles of snow on the ground, it was slow going, but Natalie finally made it to the supermarket. After finding what she needed, she walked back home, only this time she went past Leo's house. She was hoping she'd see him outside, shoveling the front walk, but he wasn't there.

Natalie stood in front of Leo's house, teeth chattering, wondering what to do. She wanted to talk to him about Saturday night and had been planning to do it this morning at school. But the snowstorm had changed that. She could probably wait until tomorrow, but she didn't want to. She wanted to talk to Leo today.

Should she just walk up to his front door and ring the bell?

Then she got an idea, a great idea, and hurried home.

* * *

An hour later, Natalie was back at Leo's, holding a small shopping bag. She rang the doorbell and waited for someone to answer.

"What do you want?" a surly Leo asked when he opened the front door and saw it was her.

That wasn't the reaction Natalie had been expecting.

"Here to finish what you started on Saturday night?" he sneered.

Natalie was confused.

"How could I be such an idiot!" he raged. "I should have known you were exactly like them!"

"What are you talking about?"

"You set me up!" Leo shouted. "You had me come to that party so Claudia could have everyone laugh at me! And like an idiot, I fell for it!"

Natalie could see the hurt on Leo's face. He truly believed what he was saying. "How could you think such a thing?" she gasped.

"Was it a dare?" Leo asked. "Were you all supposed to get a fat guy to show up and I was the only sucker who fell for it?"

"That's not true!" Natalie insisted. She placed a hand on Leo's arm, but he shook it off.

"Save it! I don't want to hear it. You're just like Claudia. Mean and horrible and spiteful." Leo started to close the door in Natalie's face. "Well, you've had your laugh. Now get lost!"

Natalie stuck her foot in the door. "Please. Let me explain. Can I come in? It's freezing out here."

"No!"

"Just for a minute," Natalie begged. "One minute."

Leo grudgingly held the door open and Natalie walked into the foyer. Instantly, she was blanketed with heat. But the look Leo gave her was just as cold as the icicles hanging from the trees.

"Start talking," Leo said. "You're running out of time."

"I didn't set you up. I swear it. I invited you to the party because I thought we could hang out together."

"Why would you want to hang out with me? I'm not blind. I have a mirror. I don't look anything like the guys you usually hang out with. I'm Blubber Boy, remember?"

"I don't care what you look like! I just want to be friends with you!"

"Why?"

"I don't know!" Natalie exclaimed. "I like talking with you! And you're great with Bonnie. I've enjoyed the time we've spent together. That's how people become friends. By spending more time with each other. That's all I wanted to do. Become your friend." Natalie checked her watch. "My minute's up. I'll go."

She turned to leave but Leo put a hand on her shoulder, stopping her.

"Do you think it's easy being me?" he asked in a soft voice. "Having people laugh at me? Point at me? Make fun of me? You don't know what it's like."

Suddenly, Natalie wanted to confess to Leo about her past. She wanted to tell him that she *did* know what it was like. But she was afraid. She'd never told anyone in North Ridge her secret before. Instead, she faced him and said, "Would I be here if I wasn't sorry?"

"Maybe you're setting me up again."

"Do you honestly believe that?"

Leo sighed, running a hand through his curls. "I don't know what to believe. Stuff like this has happened to me before."

"Leo, I *am* sorry. It wasn't a joke. If you don't believe me, ask Jennifer Harris. She can tell you how upset I was. I wanted to run after you, but she told me not to. She told me you needed some time alone. I guess I should have given you a couple more days, huh?"

"I went to that party on Saturday night because I trusted you," Leo admitted. "Because I wanted to be your friend."

"We can still be friends," Natalie said. "If you want."

"Apology accepted," Leo said.

Natalie smiled. Leo's words were the sweetest ones she'd ever heard.

"That's not the only reason I came by," she said.

"It's not?"

Natalie held up her shopping bag. "I thought we could have that movie marathon."

Natalie held her breath, waiting for Leo's answer.

"Follow me!" he exclaimed.

Eden knew she should be using her snow day to catch up on her studying. Instead, she was cleaning out her bedroom closet. The spring sales would be starting soon and she needed to make some room.

She began pulling out sweaters, dresses, skirts, tops, and jeans. What was the rule? If you only wore it once, get rid of it!

Forty-five minutes later, Eden had much more space in her closet and a pile of clothes on her bedroom floor. Her father would flip out if he saw how much stuff she was getting rid of. Good thing he was at work!

Eden was closing her closet door when a flash of white in the far corner caught her eye. She reached in and pulled out her ice skates. She couldn't remember the last time she'd used them. Maybe a year ago? She wondered if they still fit. She kicked off her sneakers and slipped her feet into them. They did!

For three years she had gone for weekly lessons, and even had competed in some amateur-level competitions, but then gave up the lessons because she grew tired of having to practice every day and on the weekends.

Staring at the skates, Eden wondered if she still knew her way around the ice.

There was only one way to find out.

Even though it had snowed, DeVille's was open. And Jennifer was stuck working. Mrs. Hudson had called that morning and asked if she could come in for a few hours. Caught off guard,

Jennifer hadn't been able to think of an excuse. So, instead of enjoying her day off like everyone else, she was standing behind a cash register. She hadn't had one customer the entire morning. Luckily, she was only working until one o'clock.

Deciding she needed to do *something* to keep herself busy, Jennifer began dusting the shelves that held the wedding favors. She had just finished with the first shelf when she felt a tap on her shoulder. She turned around with a professional smile, expecting to find a customer.

It was Will.

"What are you doing here?" she asked in surprise.

"I was riding up on the escalator and saw you. I need to buy a suit."

"For the dance?" Jennifer asked, suddenly realizing she hadn't given any thought to what she'd be wearing.

"Something like that," Will answered.

"DeVille's has a great men's department. If you don't mind sticking around, I can help you." After all, he was dressing for her. Why not get a sneak peek and steer him away from any fashion disasters? The last thing she wanted was him showing up wearing a suit with sneakers! Or a suit with a T-shirt! "I get off in half an hour. Can you wait?"

Relief washed over Will's face. "That would be great. I don't know anything about fancy clothes."

Thirty minutes later, Jennifer was going through the racks in the men's department, collecting shirts, ties, and suits.

"Let's start with these," she said, handing the pile to Will. "And remember, whatever we buy, you have to wear dress shoes! No sneakers!"

"How'd it go with the dress?" he asked as he stepped into a dressing room and pulled the blue curtain closed.

"I returned it yesterday. No questions were asked. But that's the last time I do something stupid like that."

"Until you tangle with Claudia again," Will teased as he came out wearing the first combo of shirt, suit, and tie that Jennifer had suggested.

"I don't like the shirt and tie together. The colors clash." She pushed him back into the dressing room. "Go change."

After much mixing and matching, Will went with a charcoal gray suit, a white shirt, and a black tie decorated with tiny red hearts.

"Are you sure these hearts don't look dippy?" Will asked as he walked out of the dressing room in his own clothes.

"They look classy!"

At the cash register, Jennifer insisted on letting Will use her employee discount.

"You don't have to do that."

"I know I don't, but I want to. It's the least I can do. After all, you're helping me out."

"Thanks."

After Will paid for his purchase, they left DeVille's and walked outside. The streets were piled high with snowbanks although the sidewalks had been cleared.

"Guess I won't be getting that motorcycle ride today," Jennifer said.

"'Fraid not."

They started down the block, walking side by side. Even though the snow was gone, the sidewalk was slippery in spots.

"I feel like I'm about to fall on my butt," Jennifer joked.

Seconds later, Jennifer slipped on a patch of ice. She tried to regain her balance, but couldn't. As she fell, Will tried to catch her, but slipped as well and they both crashed to the ground.

Jennifer fell first, with Will landing on top of her.

They were face-to-face, with their lips only inches apart.

Staring into Will's blue eyes, Jennifer was unaware of the hard ground or the cold snow seeping into the back of her jacket.

All she was aware of was Will's lips.

They were temptingly close.

She wanted to lift her head up and wrap her hands around his head, weave her fingers through his long, silky hair, drawing him close as she pressed her lips against his.

They looked so soft.

And kissable!

Where were these thoughts coming from? Had she suffered a concussion? She wasn't supposed to be falling for Will. This was all pretend!

But she wanted to kiss him!

And Will *had* said that they should kiss.

As research.

Did she dare?

She wasn't the kind of girl who usually made the first move. She always let the guy do that.

Although she did know how to send out signals.

Jennifer stared into Will's eyes, trying to telegraph her thoughts.

Come on, Will! Take charge. Kiss me. Kiss me!

But he didn't.

Instead, he jumped off her and pulled her back on her feet.

"Are you okay?" he asked, wiping snow off her jacket before collecting his shopping bags.

"I'm fine," she assured him.

Although I would have been better if you'd kissed me!

"We better take things slow," Will said as they started walking again.

Slow was *not* what Jennifer wanted.

Eden was in the middle of doing a figure eight when she heard her name called.

"Eden!"

She looked across the pond where she was ice-skating and saw a little girl waving at her. At first she didn't recognize her, she was so bundled up. But then, when her name was called again, she recognized the voice. It was Dexter's little sister, Yvonne.

"Hi, sweetie," she said, skating over to her. "Are you here by yourself?"

Yvonne shook her head. "Everyone else is coming."

Seconds later, Dexter, Angie, and Thelma walked out of the woods, ice skates tossed over their shoulders.

"Look who's here!" Yvonne called out, her voice filled with excitement.

"I didn't know you ice-skated," Dexter said as he sat on a bench by the side of the pond and put on his skates, lacing them up.

"I haven't in awhile. I was cleaning out my closet and found my old skates. I thought I'd give it a whirl."

"And?"

"I've still got it," Eden proudly said.

"Let's see."

Eden skated back onto the ice and did another figure eight. Then she did a double axel.

"You're just like the skaters on TV!" Yvonne exclaimed.

Eden shook her head. "I'm nowhere near as good as they are."

"Yes, you are," Yvonne stubbornly said as she stepped onto the ice, her ankles wobbly. "And you're prettier, too!"

"How are you on the ice?" Eden asked Dexter.

Angie laughed. "If they gave grades for ice-skating, Dexter would get an F!"

"You mean Dexter *isn't* perfect at everything?" Eden teased.

"When it comes to ice-skating, Mr. Perfect is Mr. Imperfect," Thelma added.

"I skate better than Dexter!" Yvonne called out as she zigzagged between the other skaters on the pond.

"No fair," Dexter grumbled, carefully stepping onto the ice. "These three pick on me all the time. They don't need you helping them."

"How about I give you some lessons?" Eden asked. "Let me be the tutor for a change."

"I'm all yours," Dexter said as his sisters abandoned them.

"Skate for me," Eden said. "Let me see your moves."

Eden cringed as she watched Dexter shuffle across the ice. She kept expecting him to fall flat on his face.

"Don't look down," she instructed him. "Keep your head up, your back straight, and yours arms out."

Eden watched as Dexter did what she told him. Instantly, she saw an improvement.

"Very good," she said as she skated alongside him. "Let your feet do the work. Watch me."

Eden glided smoothly across the ice, picking up speed, keeping one leg out behind her. Even though she didn't have any music, she decided to do one of her old routines, complete with jumps and spins. She didn't know why, but she wanted to show Dexter that she was good at *something*. That she wasn't just a mindless cheerleader who cried over her ex-boyfriends.

When she was finished, she skated over to Dexter. The look of amazement on his face was priceless.

"Wow!" he exclaimed. "Yvonne was right. You *are* better than those skaters on TV."

"I told you!" Yvonne piped up, clapping madly. "She's an ice princess."

For the rest of the afternoon, Eden divided her time between Dexter and his sisters, giving them all pointers. Dexter fell on his butt a couple of times, causing his sisters to laugh, but he was a good sport about it. He always pulled himself back up, blushing with embarrassment, and then started skating again. He also wasn't afraid to ask

Eden what he was doing wrong. Only when it started to get dark did they realize they had lost track of time.

"We've been out here all afternoon," Dexter said as he unlaced his skates.

"I've got so much homework left to do," Eden groaned. "And I still have to figure out what I'm going to do with all those clothes I'm getting rid of."

"You're getting rid of clothes?" Angie asked.

"A lot of it is stuff I've hardly worn," Eden said. A thought popped into her head. "Want to come over and see if there's anything you'd like to have?"

Angie could barely contain her excitement. "You mean it?"

"Sure."

"I can't wait!" She happily clapped her hands. "You're one of the best-dressed girls at North Ridge High."

Eden laughed. "Says who?"

"Dexter!" Yvonne loudly announced.

Eden hadn't expected to hear that! "You pay attention to what I'm wearing?" she asked in amusement.

Dexter blushed.

"Dexter always notices pretty girls," Thelma said. "Mama says he's girl-crazy."

Yvonne nodded. "Last week, he said —"

Dexter cut Yvonne off. "If we don't start hurrying, we're going to be late for dinner. Less talking and more walking," he sternly ordered.

"Will you come over for dinner, Eden?" Yvonne asked, taking Eden's hand in hers. "Please?"

"We owe you," Thelma said. "For helping us on the ice."

"Not to mention the clothes you're going to give me," Angie added.

Eden knew she should say no. She had to get home. But how could she resist the pleading looks on Dexter's sisters' faces, especially Yvonne's? And then Dexter surprised her by saying, "We'd love to have you." He crossed his heart. "I promise not to quiz you on vocabulary words."

"Okay," she told them, surrendering to their invitation, "I'll come over. But I can't stay very long."

The other reason why she said yes was because she couldn't forget what Yvonne had said.

Dexter thought she was one of the best-dressed girls at North Ridge High.

Interesting.

Very interesting . . .

"Wouldn't it be nice if people decorated for Valentine's Day like they decorated for Christmas?" Natalie asked as she and Leo walked down her block. "There could be blinking pink and red lights and cupids on front lawns. Maybe even animated boxes of chocolate where the lids lift up and some of the chocolates inside could be squished!"

"It'll never happen."

"Why not?"

"Valentine's Day isn't a holiday that includes everybody, if you know what I mean. It's aimed toward couples. Single people get left out. Why would they want to decorate for a holiday that excludes them?"

"Oh! I never thought of it that way."

"Since you're coupled," Leo said, "what are you doing on Valentine's Day? Going to the dance?"

"I guess."

"What do you mean you guess? Hasn't Tom asked you?"

Natalie didn't want to admit that Tom *hadn't* asked her yet. She was sure Leo would find that strange. But it wasn't like she was upset. Tom was going to ask her eventually. After all, they were dating. Who else was he going to ask?

Although what did it say about her that this was the first time she was thinking about Tom not asking her to dance?

"Of course he has," Natalie told Leo. "What about you?"

"Same thing as tonight. Babysitting Bonnie."

Their movie marathon had been interrupted when Lisa had called and asked Leo if he could come over and watch Bonnie. When Leo told Natalie the news, she offered to go with him. They'd brought along the DVDs they hadn't had a chance to watch and were hoping Bonnie would fall asleep early.

"Let me pop inside," Natalie said as they neared her house. "I was at the mall yesterday and bought something for Bonnie."

"A bribe couldn't hurt," Leo said. "Lisa said she's been cranky all day. She thinks she might be coming down with something."

"Poor baby."

"I'll see you in a little bit," Leo said as he continued to his brother's house.

Up in her bedroom, Natalie found the tiny stuffed monkey she had bought for Bonnie. As she was walking through the kitchen to use the back door, she saw the light on the answering machine was blinking. She hit the PLAY button and was surprised to hear Tom's voice fill the kitchen.

"Hey, Nat. Just wondering what you were up to. I thought if you were home, I'd swing by, but you're not. Give me a call when you get this message. Maybe we can still do something."

Natalie hit the ERASE button.

Even though she'd gotten Tom's message, that didn't mean she had to call him back now. After all, she was babysitting. She was busy.

She'd call him later tonight before she went to bed.

Chapter Thirteen

"And the nominees for Most Romantic Couple are . . ."

It was lunchtime and Jennifer was listening to Principal Hicks's nasal voice over the school announcement system. He always sounded stuffed up, like he had a cold.

"This is it," Violet whispered, squeezing Jennifer's arm and crossing her fingers on both hands.

"The first couple competing is Claudia Monroe and Chase Stewart."

Duh. No surprise there. Jennifer looked across the cafeteria at Claudia's table. As expected, Claudia had a smug smile on her face. Chase was sitting by her side, holding his arms up in victory.

"The second couple is Celia Armstrong and Freddy Keenan."

Now that made sense. Everyone at North Ridge High knew the story of Celia and Freddy's romance. Freddy had been crushing on Celia for months, and when he pulled her name for the Secret Santa exchange, he thought he had the perfect opportunity to show her his true feelings. Until he found out that Celia was crushing on Jake Morrisey. Because he wanted Celia to be happy, he asked Jake to pretend to be Celia's Secret Santa and take credit for the gifts he'd been leaving. But on the night of the Christmas dance, Celia figured out the truth, went straight to Freddy's house, and told him the only Secret Santa she wanted was *him*. They had been a couple ever since.

"The third couple is Noelle Kramer and Ryan Grant."

No surprise again. Noelle and Ryan had been living next door to each other for years. While Noelle had a crush on Ryan's older brother, Charlie, Ryan had a crush on her. It had taken the Secret Santa exchange to show Noelle that she had been crushing on the wrong Grant brother.

"Only two more couples to go," Violet whispered.

"I know," Jennifer nervously said. "What if he doesn't call our names?" She could just imagine the way Claudia would rub it in. Ugh!

"The fourth couple is Jennifer Harris and Will Sinclair."

Jennifer couldn't help it. She screamed. She and Will had been nominated. *They had been nominated!*

"You did it!" Violet happily cried, tossing her arms around Jennifer.

As Jennifer hugged Violet back, she stared across the cafeteria. She couldn't help it. She wanted to see the look on Claudia's face. As she expected, it wasn't happy. Claudia looked mad.

What's the matter, Claudia? Jennifer wanted to call out. *Afraid of a little competition?*

"And the last couple competing for Most Romantic is Natalie Bauer and Tom Marland," Principal Hicks finished. "Good luck to all the nominees. Let the voting begin!"

★ ★ ★

Natalie was in shock.

How had she and Tom been nominated?

She hadn't submitted an essay.

Unless . . .

Unless Tom had?

"We're in! In!" Tom exclaimed, rushing up to Natalie's side. He pulled her out of her seat and lifted her up in a hug, whirling her around in the air.

"Tom!" Natalie laughed. "Put me down! You're making me dizzy."

"Your wish is my command," Tom said as he put her feet back on the ground. "Are you surprised?"

"Uh . . . yeah! Did you submit an essay?"

"Of course I did. You didn't think I was going to let Chase walk away with another victory, did you?" He punched Chase in the arm playfully. "Get ready for a fight!"

"You're going down!" Chase exclaimed.

"Why didn't you tell me you were writing an essay?"

Tom shrugged. "If we got nominated, I wanted it to be a surprise," he explained. "And if we didn't, well, you never would have known what I'd done."

"Do you have a copy of the essay?" Natalie asked, curious to see what Tom had written. "I'd love to read it."

Tom reached into his back pocket and pulled out a folded piece of paper.

Natalie read the essay. It was sweet. A little too sweet. Tom made it sound like they were the perfect couple who never had fights or disagreements. He made it sound like they were joined at the hip and spent all their time together, and when they weren't together, they were constantly calling or text messaging each other because they couldn't stand to be apart. He also mentioned Claudia and Chase, saying that he and Natalie were best friends with them, and because of that friendship, they had been friends with each other first and then started dating. He finished the essay by saying he hoped they'd be together as long as Claudia and Chase.

"What do you think?" Tom asked.

Natalie didn't know what to say. This wasn't them. Maybe this was how Tom saw their relationship, but she didn't. She pulled him off to one side so they'd have some privacy.

"Are we a couple?" she asked.

"What do you mean?"

"We've never used the word boyfriend and girlfriend. We've never said we were exclusive."

"Yes, we're a couple! Why? Is there someone else you want to go out with?" Tom asked, his voice filled with panic.

"Of course not!" Natalie shook her head. "I guess I'm having a hard time taking all this in. You caught me off guard." She held up the essay. "I didn't know you felt this way. It's kind of intense."

"Okay, I'll admit I laid it on a little bit thick, but I had to if we were going to get nominated. And it worked! We made the final cut!" He glanced over Natalie's shoulder at Chase. "Now all we have to do is win!"

"In your dreams, Marland!" Chase hooted before Tom went running after him.

He had laid it on a little bit thick? *Did that mean Tom* didn't *mean the things he wrote*? Natalie wondered.

Was this just another competition that he was determined to win?

She also wondered something else.

If Tom had asked her to write their essay, what would she have said?

Because when she thought of them, *romantic* was the last word that came to her mind.

At the sight of Will standing at the entrance of the cafeteria, Jennifer raced over to him. "Will! Will! Did you hear? We've been nominated!"

Will made a fist and pulled his arm down. "Yes!" He gave Jennifer a smug smile. "Guess that essay worked, huh?"

Jennifer ignored his gloating. "Now that we've been nominated, all we have to do is win!"

"I don't know about that," Will said, loud enough for the students around them to hear. He closed the distance between himself and Jennifer, wrapping his arms around her waist.

"What do you mean?"

"It doesn't matter if we're voted Most Romantic, because I'm already a winner." He pulled her closer. "Want to know why?"

Jennifer sensed Will was up to something, but not sure what. "Why?"

"Because you're my girlfriend."

And then before Jennifer knew what was happening, Will leaned his face into hers and gave her a kiss. Automatically, her arms wrapped around him, pulling him close as their lips melded together. Behind her, she could hear students hooting and hollering. There were shouts of "More! More!"

Will broke the kiss and placed a finger on Jennifer's lips. "See you after school."

A dazed Jennifer watched Will leave as Violet rushed up to her side.

"What was it like?" she frantically asked. "What was it like?"

"Incredible," Jennifer whispered.

His kiss had been unlike any kiss she'd ever had before. She'd *felt* it throughout her entire body. His lips had devoured hers and she'd loved every second of it.

"Did you guys discuss kissing?" Violet asked softly.

"It came up once, but we never talked about it again."

"Well, correct me if I'm wrong," Violet said, "but I think it just became part of the deal!"

When Natalie went back to her lunch table, she found an angry Claudia waiting. Great. *Just* what she needed.

"Aren't you full of surprises?" Claudia said, her voice dripping with acid. "Keeping more secrets from me?"

"Okay, Claudia, withdraw the fangs," Eden said, coming to Natalie's defense. "There's no need for your special brand of venom. Didn't you hear Tom? He's the one who submitted the essay. Natalie knew nothing about it."

"So she says."

Natalie found herself getting angry. "Are you calling me a liar?"

"This wouldn't be the first time you've lied to me."

"I've never lied to you!"

"You didn't tell me about Jennifer and Will."

"Because Jennifer asked me not to! That's not lying!"

"You're supposed to be my friend, not hers!"

"I *am* your friend!" Natalie exclaimed. *Although sometimes I wonder why!* "What do you want me to do, Claudia? Tom and I have been nominated. I can't change that."

"Don't expect to win," Claudia said. "Chase and I have been together since freshman year. We're the most romantic couple at North Ridge High. No one is going to beat us."

"I'll be the first one applauding when you get crowned," Natalie said before leaving to buy her lunch. *Unless I bash you with your crown because you're so obnoxious!*

"Congratulations," Leo said as they both grabbed a lunch tray and stepped into the hot-food line.

"Thanks," she said glumly.

Leo frowned. "You don't sound too happy."

"Tom didn't tell me he was submitting us for the contest. I was totally surprised when our names were announced."

"Don't think you're romantic enough?" Leo joked as he started loading his tray.

"If you want to know the truth, no, I don't." Natalie selected a veggie burger. "And then there's Claudia."

"What's her damage?"

"She's having a major hissy fit because Tom and I are competing against her. Even though she didn't say it, I know she thinks I stabbed her in the back."

"Don't feel bad. Lots of people would *love* to do that."

As they approached the cash register, Natalie couldn't help but notice how much food was on Leo's tray. She opened her mouth, but then closed it.

"Did you want to say something?" Leo asked.

Natalie shook her head.

"Come on," Leo urged. "You can say it."

Natalie pointed to his lunch tray. "It's none of my business, but are you really going to eat all that?"

"What can I say? I'm a growing boy. I'm hungry."

"There's nothing wrong with eating a lot, so long as you're eating healthy," Natalie said. "You've got *a lot* of carbs on your tray. And a lot of fried food. Some veggies wouldn't hurt."

"Any other suggestions?"

"You could exercise a little."

Leo made a face. "Exercise and I don't go well together. I'm sure you can figure out my least favorite class of the day."

"Gym?"

"Always chosen last no matter what we're playing. Can't say that I blame them, I'm so out of shape."

"You could change that."

"How?"

"It's always easier exercising with a friend. Why don't you come jogging with me tomorrow morning."

"Me? Jog? Are you crazy?"

"Just try it once. If you don't like it, I'll never ask again."

Leo thought about it as he put back the two slices of pizza that were on his tray and replaced them with a bowl of steamed baby carrots.

"Okay, I'll try it *once*. Tomorrow morning in front of my house?"

"Great!" Natalie exclaimed. "It's a date!"

Chapter Fourteen

After school, Eden was waiting for Dexter in the school library. As she flipped through her SAT study guide, she couldn't help thinking of Claudia and Natalie and how they were both going to be competing for Most Romantic Couple. She wondered if Keith hadn't broken up with her, if they would have also been competing. She probably would have written an essay for the contest and done nothing but talk about how great she thought he was.

Eden slammed closed her study guide, angry with herself. Why was she thinking about Keith? It was over between them! And he wasn't great. He was a jerk!

Looking around the library and seeing all the decorations that were up — all the pink and red hearts and cupids with arrows — she knew why she was thinking of him. Valentine's Day. Everywhere she turned, inside and outside of school, she was reminded that *love* was in the air. There was no escaping it.

This Thursday everyone was going to have a valentine but her.

She dreaded going to the Valentine's Day dance. If she could skip it, she would, but she knew Claudia would go ballistic if she didn't show up. She expected her to be there when she and Chase were announced as Most Romantic Couple.

Claudia was *so* sure that she and Chase were going to win. Okay, they had been together since freshman year, but were they in love? Wasn't that what this contest was about? Love and romance and how you felt about the person you were with? Sometimes Eden felt like Claudia and Chase were a couple because Claudia was one of the most popular girls at school and Chase was one of the most popular guys and they had decided to fuse their popularity together so they could become *super* popular.

That wasn't love.

Love was being with that one person who made you feel like no one else did. Who made you laugh and smile. Who shared private jokes and memories with you. Who you could talk to without saying a word and who was always there when you needed them. Who made you feel safe. Secure. Special.

At least that's what Eden had always heard. Maybe she was reading too many Danielle Steel novels and watching too many Lifetime movies. Did it matter? After all, Claudia wasn't going to be alone on Valentine's Day. *She* was.

"What's wrong? You look sad. Did you run into another ex-boyfriend?"

Eden looked up and saw Dexter taking off his book bag.

Eden sighed. "I'm just feeling sorry for myself. My friends Claudia and Natalie and their boyfriends have been nominated for Most Romantic Couple and I was thinking how I don't have a boyfriend."

"Yet," Dexter corrected as he sat down.

"Yet?"

"In a couple of weeks, you'll be going out with someone new."

"How do you know that?"

Dexter reached into his book bag for his SAT study guide. "Girls like you always have boyfriends."

Eden didn't know why, but Dexter's comment bugged her. "What do mean, *girls like me*? That sounded like an insult!"

Dexter held his hands up in surrender. "It wasn't! Eden, you're a knockout. What guy wouldn't want to go out with you?"

"If I'm such a knockout, why do my boyfriends keep dumping me?" Eden bitterly asked. "Why do they keep breaking up with me?"

Dexter was silent for a minute. Then he pulled out a piece of paper and a pencil. "Let's look at this logically. What's the common denominator?"

"Me."

Dexter wrote down Eden's name. "And what are the other factors of the equation?"

"The guys?"

Dexter added their names. "What do the guys all have in common?"

"Other than dumping me?"

"Be serious! Think!"

"They're all jocks."

"And?"

"Maybe there's something wrong with me and I don't know it?"

Dexter shook his head. "Why did you go out with Malcolm, Luther, and Keith in the first place?

"Because they asked me out."

"That was it?"

"Well, they were all hotties!"

Dexter rolled his eyes.

"What?" Eden asked. "Looks matter! You have to be attracted to the person you're with!"

"Nothing more?"

"I don't think so."

"How about when you were dating? What was that like?"

Eden gave it some thought. "We always had a hard time figuring out what to do. We could never make plans and when we did, it was usually what the other person wanted to do, not both of us. And we went out on a lot of group dates. We never had a lot of alone time."

Dexter nodded knowingly.

"Have you figured out what went wrong?" Eden asked. "If you have, tell me! My dating life is at stake!"

"You didn't have anything in common with

those guys. That's why things fizzled out. You didn't get to know them first." Dexter's face became serious. "When you were out with other couples, that lack of connection didn't matter because the group dynamic propelled the relationship, but when you were alone, there was nothing to sustain the interpersonal development between you and the guy you were dating."

"Wow!" Eden exclaimed. "You sound like a textbook!"

"I'll simplify it," Dexter said. "Just because a couple looks good together doesn't mean they *are* good together. A couple needs to have the same interests."

"Not necessarily," Eden argued. "Opposites attract."

"True," Dexter conceded. "But they need to have *something* in common."

"I guess," Eden grudgingly admitted.

"Who do you think is going to be voted Most Romantic?"

"Claudia and Chase. They're the most popular couple at North Ridge High."

"Being the most popular doesn't mean they're the most romantic."

"But it does guarantee them a lot of votes," Eden pointed out.

"Does it?" Dexter asked. "I'd like to believe in true love winning."

Eden did a double take, not believing her ears. "*You* believe in true love?"

"Now I'm the one who's insulted!" Dexter exclaimed, although his tone of voice was teasing. "Why do you find that so hard to believe?"

Eden shrugged. "I guess I've never thought of you as the type. Love is so emotional and, well, *messy*, and you're always so quiet and reserved."

"That's why you should never judge a book by its cover," Dexter said. "And speaking of books . . ." He held up his SAT study guide. "Let's get cracking!"

Eden opened up her book and turned to the page Dexter wanted to start with. As she did, she studied him out of the corner of her eye. Who would have thought he believed in true love? He was full of surprises.

And then she remembered what he had said earlier.

She'd been so angry, she hadn't paid any attention.

But now his words came back to her.

He thought she was a knockout!

And then she remembered what Angie and Yvonne had told her yesterday. He thought she was one of the best-dressed girls at North Ridge High.

A crazy thought popped into her head.

Was Dexter interested in her?

But it didn't make any sense! He was a straight A, honor roll, Advanced Placement student who was in the chess club and on the school debate team. She was a cheerleader who needed a tutor! Talk about a cliché! They'd be the perfect couple for that reality show, *Beauty and the Geek.*

And yet she had just told him that opposites attracted . . .

But still! Dexter had *never* given her any sort of clue that he was interested in her. He'd never flirted with her or looked her over from head to toe the way most guys did. Back at his house the night before, she had spent most of her time with his sisters. They hadn't been alone at all. She *knew* when a guy was interested, and Dexter had never given her that vibe.

Even though he had said those nice things about her — and he'd thoughtfully given her those tulips — there hadn't been any sort of hidden meaning.

Had there?

No! There hadn't!

She was imagining things.

Yes, that's what it was. It was all in her head. She was so desperate to have a boyfriend and not be alone on Valentine's Day that she was imagining that Dexter wanted to go out with her.

Chapter Fifteen

"How hard can it be to make a couple dozen cookies?" Jennifer asked as she and Violet unloaded the ingredients they had bought at the local grocery store after school. "You toss all the ingredients in a bowl, mix them up, plop the dough on a cookie sheet, and then pop it into the oven."

"*Sounds* easy enough," Violet murmured. "But you know me, Jennifer. I can't even boil water."

"You're worrying too much!"

Sheba came running into the kitchen at the sound of the rustling bags, dancing between Jennifer and Violet's legs. "Shoo, Sheba," Jennifer told her. "I don't have anything for you."

Sheba meowed and sat down, staring up at Jennifer with pleading eyes.

"Go away," Jennifer told her. "I'm busy."

Sheba meowed again and then darted under the kitchen table.

"Why are we making these cookies again?" Violet asked as she opened a box of eggs.

"We have to beat Claudia at her own game," Jennifer said as she reached into a kitchen cabinet for a measuring cup. "Did you see the way she wallpapered the entire school?"

By the time the bell for the last class had rung, flyers for Claudia and Chase were on all the walls at North Ridge High. Some said: VOTE FOR CLAUDIA AND CHASE. Others said: CLAUDIA AND CHASE: THE FIRST COUPLE OF ROMANCE, while another batch said: CLAUDIA + CHASE = LOVE. And the flyers didn't just have type on them. There were also photos of Claudia and Chase on them.

"I heard she's throwing a party on Saturday night if they win, and everyone at school is invited," Violet said.

"Oooh, she's so sneaky!" Jennifer fumed. "If they don't win, then there's no party. So everyone knows the only way to get a party is if they vote for Claudia and Chase!"

"Let's give our classmates a little credit," Violet said as she searched through Jennifer's mother's collection of cookbooks over the stainless-steel refrigerator. "A lot of them can't stand Claudia. I'm sure they'll be giving their votes to one of the other couples."

"Hopefully Will and me!" Jennifer exclaimed. "Did you find a cookie recipe?"

Violet nodded as she walked over with an open cookbook. Jennifer had decided to bake heart-shaped sugar cookies with her initials and Will's on them, handing them out at school tomorrow. Kind of like an early Valentine's Day treat. It couldn't hurt. Nothing said lovin' like something from the oven! At least that's what her grandmother claimed.

"This sounds easy," Jennifer said as she skimmed the recipe and began cracking eggs into a mixing bowl. "Let's get started! I can't wait for the kitchen to fill with the sweet smell of baking cookies!"

Two hours later, the smell of burning cookies was thick in the air.

"What did we do wrong this time?" Jennifer wailed as she put on an oven mitt and pulled a tray of burned cookies out of the oven.

Violet peered at the oven temperature. "Oops! I accidentally set the oven for four hundred and seventy-five degrees instead of three hundred and seventy-five degrees."

Jennifer emptied the tray of cookies into a garbage bag where there were already four other disastrous batches.

"We'll get it right this time," Jennifer insisted just as there was a knock on the back door. When she opened it, she found Will waiting. He made a face as he walked into the kitchen. "What's that horrible smell?"

"Our cookies," Violet answered.

"Cookies?"

Jennifer watched as Will glanced around the kitchen. It was a disaster area. There were used bowls filling the sink, scattered piles of cracked eggshells, as well as opened bags of flour and sugar spilling across the counters and onto the floor. She and Violet didn't look that hot, either. They were covered with a light dusting of flour from when they'd tried to open the bag and it had exploded in their faces.

Will pointed to a platter filled with some cookies. "Those look edible," he said.

"Don't!" Jennifer cried out.

But it was too late. Will had already bitten into an unfrosted cookie. As soon as he did, he instantly spat it out into his hand.

"Blech!"

"That was the batch where Violet added half a cup of salt instead of sugar," Jennifer explained.

"I got confused!" Violet cried. "The type in the cookbook was too small!"

"What's wrong with those?" Will asked, pointing to a plate of cookies sitting in a soupy white liquid.

"I frosted those before the cookies had cooled," Jennifer added. "The icing melted off. And they're too soft. I think we forgot to add baking powder."

"Why are you baking cookies?" Will asked.

"Jennifer wants to hand them out at school," Violet explained. "She's going to frost them and put your initials and hers on them."

"I thought you wanted to win this," Will said, looking around the kitchen again and shaking his head in disbelief.

"I do!" Jennifer exclaimed.

"Then it looks like I'm going to have to help you out. Otherwise we're going to *lose* votes!"

Will left and returned from the grocery store with fresh supplies, whipping up a new batch of cookie batter without even needing to look at a cookbook.

"How did you know how to do that?" Jennifer asked as he placed two filled cookie sheets into the oven.

"I'm a guy of many talents," Will said. "You just don't know what they are yet."

I know you're a great kisser, Jennifer thought, remembering his kiss at lunch. Then she chased the thought away. Will hadn't meant the kiss. He'd been doing it for show.

Still, he *knew* how to kiss! She didn't think she'd ever felt a kiss the way she had when Will kissed her.

Will squinted at her. "You have a funny look on your face."

Jennifer blushed. "I was daydreaming."

"You also have some flour on your nose." Will moved closer to Jennifer, closing the distance between them. He lifted a finger and lightly brushed it across Jennifer's nose. "And on your cheeks." He then brushed a finger over Jennifer's cheek. "Your lips, too."

As Will ran a finger over Jennifer's lower lip, she felt like saying, *Why don't you kiss it off?*

ıd, Will stared at her. He
:lf. Like he didn't know

ınifer thought. *I wouldn't*
'

didn't say that, Jennifer
cookie batter and then
me on, confess," she said
er. "Where did you learn

ı. My mom and grand-
:en bakers. When I was
: kitchen with them. A lot
u pick it up. And I watch

a chef someday?" Violet

. "Who knows? It's fun
of different ingredients
ether to see what you can

?" Jennifer asked as she

ds on a dish towel. "No
:ighborhood and wanted
ny thoughts about our

"I say we keep doing what we've been doing. It seems to be working."

Will nodded. "Okay." He pointed to the bowls of cookie batter that he'd made. "All you have to do is keep popping these into the oven when you take out the other batches. Let them cool for at least an hour before frosting them." He slipped his motorcycle jacket back on and headed for the back door. "Think you can handle that?"

Jennifer wanted to play dumb and say she wasn't sure. That maybe he should stick around until all the cookies were made. But before she could say anything, Violet exclaimed, "Of course we can! Right, Jen?"

"Right," Jennifer reluctantly said as she watched Will say good night and walk out the back door.

Will's cookies were perfect. Jennifer and Violet were frosting the first batch when Violet asked, "What's wrong?"

"Nothing's wrong," Jennifer said as she added a dab of frosting to a cookie and spread it out.

"Don't lie to me. I can tell. What is it?"

Jennifer finished frosting the cookie and

started on another one. "Well," she admitted, "I was wondering about something."

"What?"

"Why didn't he kiss me again?"

"That's easy," Violet explained. "No audience."

"Oh yeah, right." That confirmed what she had originally thought. The kiss he'd given her at lunch didn't mean anything. "But I was getting the sense that he wanted to kiss me again and held himself back. Unless I was just imagining it."

"Why would you have imagined it?" Violet asked, confused. "Something's not making sense. You sound almost *bummed* that he didn't kiss you again." Violet dropped the knife she was using to frost with and a look of horror washed over her face. "The only reason you'd sound bummed is if you *wanted* him to kiss you. You're not falling for him, are you?"

"Of course not!" Jennifer quickly answered.

But am I? she silently wondered.

"Jennifer!" Violet wailed. "How could you fall for the Heartbreaker? Didn't I tell you to be careful?"

"I haven't fallen for him," Jennifer snapped. "Maybe, just maybe, I have a teensy tiny crush on him. That's all."

Violet picked up her frosting knife. "Get over it! Will is your fake boyfriend. Fake! Fake! Fake! Repeat after me! Fake! Once Valentine's Day is over, this is all going to end."

"I know that," Jennifer said. "You don't have to remind me."

"I think I do," Violet said. "If I don't, you stand the risk of becoming the Heartbreaker's next victim!"

Chapter Sixteen

"Ready to go jogging?" Natalie asked when a sleepy-eyed Leo opened his front door at 7 A.M. on Wednesday morning.

Leo yawned as he walked outside and locked the front door behind him. "I'm never up this early. Usually, I'm curled under my sheets for at least another hour. Where it's toasty warm!" Leo shivered. "It's freezing out here!"

"You'll warm up once you start moving," Natalie said. She was wearing a pink jogging suit with a pink and white striped scarf around her neck and white earmuffs covering her ears. At her waist was her iPod. Usually she listened to music while she jogged, but this morning she planned on talking to Leo so she could build up his confidence.

"Please don't tell me you do this *every* day."

"Only three days a week," Natalie said as they started walking toward the park. The streetlights were turning off as the morning sun started to peek out from behind clouds, chasing away the last shadows of the night. "I wouldn't do it unless I enjoyed it. It helps me clear my head. And it's good exercise."

Leo shuddered. "The dreaded E word."

"Keep an open mind," Natalie urged. "Jogging is one of the cheapest forms of exercise. All you need is a pair of sneakers and you're ready to go."

"The only place I want to go is back to bed!" Leo exclaimed.

When they reached the park, Natalie stretched her legs and encouraged Leo to do the same. When she finished, she headed for the jogging path, making sure Leo was following.

"Ready?" she asked while jogging in place.

Leo shook his head. He had a look of panic on his face. "I can't."

"Why not?"

He pointed to the early morning joggers already on the path. "They're going to look at me. They're going to wonder what I'm doing here."

"No, they're not. They're too busy focusing on themselves. And what if they do look at you? So what? Ignore them."

"I can't."

"Yes, you can," Natalie insisted, taking Leo by the hand. She could see the fear in his eyes and she recognized it because she used to feel the same way when she was heavier. "Come on," she softly encouraged. "You can do this, Leo. I know you can."

Natalie started jogging but slowed her pace down considerably so Leo could keep up with her. They made it around the path once without stopping before Leo collapsed on a park bench, breathing heavily. "Continue without me," he wheezed, waving a hand in the air. "I'm wiped out."

"But you made it around the path once!" Natalie excitedly told him as she sat down next to him. "That's good, Leo. Very good!"

"If it's good, why do I feel so awful?" he gasped.

"Because you're out of shape. Your body isn't used to it. But little by little, it *will* get used to it. You'll be able to go around the path more often, as well as faster!"

"I'll never be as fast as them," Leo said as joggers zipped by.

"Not for awhile," Natalie agreed. "But you can do other things. Why not try power walking? You could get some hand weights and walk around the path with them. And when the weather gets warmer, we could go bicycling. Or even hiking." Natalie waited until Leo had caught his breath. Then she got to her feet and pulled him by the hand. "Let's go around one more time."

"I'm done," Leo said. "We had a deal, remember? You told me I could try it once, and if I didn't like it, you'd never ask me again."

"So that's it? You're just going to give up? You haven't even tried! I never would have thought of you as a quitter, Leo Barnes."

Leo got off the bench and faced Natalie. "Why do you care so much?"

The words were on the tip of her tongue. *Because I know what you're going through. I want to help you! I know you can do it because I did it!*

But the words wouldn't come out. She couldn't say them because she never liked thinking about the old Natalie. All she wanted to do was forget her.

to sound like a public
ɔut carrying around all
You need to do some-

ɔut of the park. "That's

ubborn?" Natalie called

ıer, throwing his hands
I don't want to get too
t to get hurt."
ıurt?"
makes any sense. You're
ıouldn't even be talking

ɪrection of North Ridge
:ks we go to every day!
you what happened on

ɪncient history. That we

of repeating itself," Leo
caught me jogging out
with a video camera and
'd be up on YouTube in

some sort of embarrassing clip. Imagine what your friends would say then."

"I don't care what anyone says," Natalie told Leo. "You're my friend. That's all that matters. Don't you want to be friends with me?"

Leo squirmed, rubbing a hand behind his neck. "We can be friends, but . . ."

"But what?"

"But I want to be more than just friends," Leo confessed.

And then, before Natalie could say or do anything, Leo pulled her into his arms and gave her a kiss.

Natalie didn't resist the kiss. She didn't push Leo away and ask what he was doing. Instead, she surrendered to his kiss, even though she knew it was wrong. She wasn't supposed to be kissing another guy! After all, she already had a boyfriend and they were competing to be North Ridge High's Most Romantic Couple!

Leo broke the kiss and pulled away from Natalie. "I shouldn't have done that," he said in a rush. "I'm sorry. But I wanted to. I had to." Leo stared down at himself. "I've never had any will-power. Obviously."

"You don't have to apologize," Natalie said. "The kiss was nice."

"You don't have to say that."

"I'm not. You're a very good kisser."

Leo seemed surprised. "I am?"

"Hasn't anyone ever told you that?"

"You're the first girl I've ever kissed," Leo confessed.

"I never would have known."

"I'm sorry," Leo said again. "I've messed up everything between us, haven't I?"

"No, you haven't," Natalie said as they walked out of the park. "We're still friends. We'll just pretend that the kiss never happened, okay?"

"Okay," Leo agreed, relief washing over his face. "It never happened."

But the kiss *did* happen, Natalie reminded herself as she walked home to get ready for school.

And she couldn't forget it.

Because Leo's kiss was *nothing* like Tom's kisses.

It was better!

When Natalie got to school, she hurried to her locker. She was running late and needed to get to her class before the bell rang. She had English first period today and Mrs. Ambrosia expected everyone in their seats the second the bell rang. If you weren't, she marked you as late and gave you a detention slip.

As she raced down the hall, she could see students pointing at her and whispering. What were they talking about? Natalie stopped in her tracks as a thought occurred to her. Panic overwhelmed her. Could someone have seen Leo kiss her? Was that what they were all whispering about?

She started walking slowly, casually turning her head to the left and right, trying to hear what they were saying, but couldn't hear anything. There was too much noise and too many conversations going on.

But she noticed something else.

A lot of the students, after staring at her, were pointing to the floor.

She looked down and was surprised to see a trail of pink paper hearts. She'd been in such a rush to get to her locker, she hadn't even noticed them.

As she followed the hearts, she saw they were leading all the way to her locker. When she got there, she found a surprise waiting.

Hanging from the handle of her locker in a tiny pink bag was a stuffed beagle holding a little sign that said BE MINE.

Her first thought was Leo. Only he would do something this sweet. A card was attached to the bag and she opened it, expecting to find Leo's signature.

But she didn't.

The puppy was from Tom.

The guilt Natalie had been struggling with since Leo kissed her returned. She had tried to ignore it, but now it was back. She should have been thrilled that Tom had done something so romantic. It must have taken him forever to paste all those hearts up the stairs and down the hallway. But he had never done anything like this before. Why now? Because tomorrow was Valentine's Day? Or was it because they were competing as Most Romantic Couple and he wanted to get votes?

She took the puppy out of the bag and stared into his droopy eyes. Why had she thought Leo was the one who had left her the puppy and not Tom?

More importantly, why did she *want* the puppy to have been from Leo?

★ ★ ★

When Natalie walked into the cafeteria at lunch, Mindy Yee grabbed her by the hand.

"You're just in time!"

"For what?" Natalie asked.

"We're going to have a little romance test!" Mindy exclaimed as she pulled Natalie to the front of the cafeteria where there were five chairs. Already sitting in them were Claudia, Jennifer, Noelle Kramer, and Celia Armstrong.

"Romance test?" Natalie repeated as Mindy pushed her into the empty chair between Jennifer and Noelle.

Mindy nodded. "To see how well the couples know each other."

"Three guesses as to whose idea this was," Jennifer whispered to Natalie.

"Claudia?"

"Uh-huh," Jennifer said. "Mindy's on the dance committee. I heard Claudia suggested it would make the competition more interesting if everyone got to know us all a little bit better."

"Next thing you know, she'll be paying people for votes," Noelle commented.

"Don't give her any ideas!" Jennifer whispered back.

"I wouldn't be surprised if Mindy slipped her the questions ahead of time," Celia added. "Remember the way she gave Amber Davenport the names of those seniors when she was in charge of the Secret Santa bag with everyone's names in it?"

Natalie did remember. Before heading off to a boarding school in Massachusetts last month — her little stunt with changing the names had blown up in her face, resulting in a very embarrassing catfight at the Secret Santa dance — Amber Davenport had been the Queen Bee of North Ridge High. Even Claudia had been afraid of her. But now that Amber was gone, Claudia had taken her place. It seemed like there was never a shortage of mean girls at North Ridge High.

But there were nice girls, too. Natalie had a class with Noelle and another with Celia. She liked them both although she had never really had a chance to hang out with them. She should do something about that.

"Okay!" Mindy announced, walking in front of them with a microphone. The cafeteria quieted down. "Now that everyone's here, let's get started. I'm going to ask the girlfriends questions and they're going to give me answers. Our freshman volunteers" — Mindy pointed to five freshman girls — "will write the answers down on cue cards. Then we're going to bring the guys back out and ask them a different set of questions. After the guys answer, the girls will lift up their cards and show their answers. Easy, right?"

Wrong! Natalie thought.

She had a bad feeling about this.

A very bad feeling.

The questions were pretty simple and straightforward: What's the one thing your boyfriend does that drives you crazy? What's something you know about him that no one else does? What's the most romantic thing he's ever done for you? What's the meanest thing he's ever done to you?

All the other girls instantly had an answer ready, but Natalie had to scramble. She didn't know what to say! How could she have been going out with Tom for a month and not know anything about him?

When the guys were brought out to the cafeteria, chairs were arranged next to the girls. When Tom sat down next to Natalie, he gave her a kiss on the cheek. "Hey, babe! Ready to rack up some points?"

Before Natalie could answer, Mindy started asking the questions again so the guys could answer. As expected, Chase answered every question correctly.

When Will answered the meanest thing question, he got a big laugh when he imitated the way Jennifer had jumped out of her seat when he'd told her to open her eyes during a scary scene at a horror movie. Jennifer, who gave the right answer, swatted him over the head with her cue card. Will answered all the other questions correctly as well, admitting that it drove Jennifer crazy when he called her Red, no one knew that he secretly liked to bake, and when it came to being romantic, he was always trying to outdo himself.

Freddy told everyone that the most romantic thing he had ever done for Celia was to ask her crush to pretend to be her Secret Santa. That got a big "awww" from all the girls. Ryan also got an "awww" when he talked about the

Secret Santa gifts he'd left for Noelle. Freddy and Ryan also answered the rest of their questions correctly.

Tom didn't do as well as the other guys. When Natalie said it drove her crazy when Tom criticized what she was wearing, he said it was when he wouldn't let her pick the movie. Natalie thought the meanest thing he'd ever done was embarrass her in front of a friend (she was thinking of Leo), while Tom felt it was showing up two hours late for a date because a football game had gone into overtime. Natalie admitted that even though Tom pretended to be a good sport, he was super competitive and hated losing. No one knew how crazy it made him, she confessed. Tom's answer was that no one knew he really liked reading poetry.

The only question Tom got right was the most romantic one. But Natalie knew they'd get that one right. How could they get it wrong? He had left the trail of hearts and stuffed puppy that morning.

"Looks like it's a four-way tie so far!" Mindy exclaimed. "Let's see what happens after Round Two!"

"We'll do better on the next round," Natalie

told Tom as she got out of her seat to follow the other girls out of the cafeteria. She could tell he was upset because they were in last place.

Tom didn't answer. He just sulked in his chair.

When it came to the second round of questions, the guys were asked: What's her favorite movie? How does she like her popcorn? Where does she see herself in ten years? What's the nicest thing she's ever done?

Claudia, like Chase, matched all her answers correctly.

Jennifer got two answers wrong. Will didn't know what her favorite movie was and he didn't know where she'd be in ten years. He did get another laugh, though, from the cafeteria when he asked her, "Aren't we still going to be together in ten years? You're not trying to tell me something, are you?" because her answer to the question hadn't been, "Happily married to Will."

Noelle and Celia also messed up on the ten-year question, although they got all the other ones right.

And Natalie got every single answer wrong.

"Looks like we have a winner!" Mindy

announced as she pointed at Claudia and Chase, who kissed. "They *are* the Most Romantic Couple at North Ridge High. Don't forget it!"

Tom threw down his cue cards and stormed out of the cafeteria. Natalie hurried after him. "Tom! Wait up!"

He stopped and whirled around, his face angry. "I can't believe the way you messed up!"

"*I* messed up?" Natalie asked in disbelief. "You gave some wrong answers, too!"

"This could cost us votes!"

"You really don't think we stand a chance of winning, do you?"

"Why not?"

Because we're not the most romantic couple at North Ridge High! Natalie wanted to scream. *Celia and Freddy are. Noelle and Ryan. Jennifer and Will. Even Claudia and Chase! Why are* we *competing to be Most Romantic when we're* not*?*

But Natalie didn't say that.

"Claudia and Chase seem to be the favorites to win," she told him.

"That doesn't mean they are. You can't think that way, Nat! If you want to be a winner, you have to think like one. You can't think like a loser!"

"I'm not thinking like a loser! I don't care if we win! It doesn't matter. Aren't I already a winner because you're my boyfriend?"

"It matters to *me*," Tom said. "And because it matters to me, it should matter to you."

Tom headed back to the first floor, leaving Natalie alone. She couldn't believe the conversation she'd just had. It was just another example of how competitive Tom could be.

He always wanted to be a winner.

But who was competitive when it came to love and romance?

If you found someone, you were already a winner.

Weren't you?

Chapter Seventeen

Jennifer couldn't believe her eyes. Was that Will buying a piece of jewelry in Bring the Bling?

She had come to the mall after school because she needed to kill some time before going to DeVille's for the early evening shift and decided to pop into some stores and see if she could find a dress for the Valentine's Day dance. She had been on her way to House of Fashion when she had caught sight of Will.

She pressed herself against the wall outside the jewelry store and peeked through the plate-glass window. She knew she shouldn't be spying on Will, but she couldn't resist. She saw him pointing to a display case and watched as a salesclerk pulled out a necklace with a pink heart-shaped crystal. Will held the necklace in his hands and then nodded to the salesclerk, who pulled out a gift box and placed the necklace in it, before walking over to the cash register.

He was buying it!

Was it a gift for Valentine's Day?

Could it be for *her*?

But they had never discussed buying each other gifts. She'd been thinking of buying Will something as a way of thanking him for agreeing to go along with her charade, but she had never expected him to buy something for her.

She ducked away from the window before Will saw her and continued walking through the mall, her head spinning.

This changed everything. Will had *never* had a girlfriend before. Why would he start now? It was too much to hope for.

But maybe, just maybe, he had developed feelings for her.

The way she had for him.

Because she hadn't been honest with Violet last night. She had more than just a teeny tiny crush on Will.

She was falling for him.

Big time.

There were times when he drove her crazy, but there were also times when he made her laugh. Underneath that bad-boy exterior, there was a sweet and considerate guy whom she wanted to spend more time with. Get to know better.

And then there were his fantastic kisses . . .

She got goose bumps remembering the way his lips had felt against hers.

She wanted Will to be her boyfriend for *real.*

That would be the best Valentine's Day gift ever.

If Will had developed feelings for her, when was he going to tell her? Should she wait for him to confess his feelings? If he was planning a surprise, she didn't want to spoil it. He was probably going to give her the necklace tomorrow night, before they went to the dance and found out if they'd been voted Most Romantic. Now, more than ever, she needed to find a great dress!

She headed straight for House of Fashion. When she arrived, the store was swarming with girls. Apparently, she wasn't the only one searching for a Valentine's Day dress. She wiggled herself between two girls who were going through a rack of dresses and started flipping through various styles and colors. Nothing was wowing her. Where was the dress that was going to make her look like a knockout?

She decided to move to another section of the store. As she walked through the crowd, she came face to face with Natalie.

"Hey!" Jennifer said, giving her a smile. "Let me guess. Shopping for a dress for the dance?"

"A new dress is the last thing I need. I'm sure I'll find something in my closet. I'm here with Claudia and Eden. They're the ones shopping."

"Claudia's here?" Jennifer decided to leave before running into her. Otherwise she was going to open her mouth and get herself into some sort of mess.

"Uh-huh. And not very happy. She's hated every dress she's tried on."

"I'll come back later. The last person I want to see is her. I'm sure she'll gloat about winning the romance test."

Natalie rolled her eyes. "That's all she's been talking about the entire afternoon."

"What did you think of it?"

"Can you say *disaster*?" Natalie asked. "Tom was *so* mad at me."

"It wasn't your fault. You guys haven't been dating very long."

"Neither have you and Will," Natalie pointed out. "Look how well the two of you did."

"Some couples mesh more quickly than others."

"I guess." Natalie sighed.

Jennifer could sense that something was bothering Natalie. "Is everything okay? Do you want to talk? I don't have to get to work for another hour. We could grab a latte in the food court."

"I'm okay. Just sorting out some personal stuff."

Jennifer wondered if that personal stuff had to do with Tom, but didn't ask.

"Things seem to be going great with you and Will," Natalie said. "I'm glad."

Jennifer could see that Natalie meant it and it made her like her even more. It also made her want to ask her a question. She couldn't ask Violet because she needed an honest answer from someone who didn't know the situation she was in.

"How can you tell if a guy really likes you?"

"Easy," Natalie said. "He'll come right out and tell you. Sometimes he'll even *show* you."

Natalie sounded like she was talking from personal experience. "He will? How?"

"He'll get physical. You know, with a kiss."

. But it hadn't been a real
e been trying to fool her?

tell you?" Jennifer asked.

ou," Natalie said. "If you
should tell him. *Especially*
like you. You know how
es. They're shy and they
at they're feeling or think-
out of them."

n?" Jennifer asked.

out it for a second and
nnifer couldn't help but
. . . happier. Like a weight
her shoulders. "I would.

lvice," Jennifer said, won-
going to do the next time

ouse of Fashion dressing
ed trying on new clothes
ut from all angles in one of
way mirrors. But today her

heart wasn't in it. She hadn't liked any of the dresses she had tried on. What did it matter what she was wearing? It wasn't like she was dressing for anyone. But Claudia had dragged her and Natalie to the mall with her, insisting that they all had to find new dresses for the Valentine's Day dance. Natalie was still outside searching through the racks, while Eden kept giving Claudia her opinion.

"What do you think of this one?" Claudia asked as she modeled in front of Eden. She was wearing a hot pink baby-doll dress.

"It's adorable," Eden said.

"I hate it!" Claudia exclaimed, ripping the dress off and hurling it at Eden. She collected a bunch of hangers with dresses she had already tried on and shoved them into Eden's arms. "And I hate these! Go hang them back up while I try on something else!"

Eden smothered a sigh. She didn't know how many more of Claudia's temper tantrums she could take. All the dresses had looked stunning on her. What did she want?

As she walked out of the dressing room, she ran into Dexter's sister Angie, who was wearing one of the outfits she'd given her. She was in a purple and black, plaid-pleated mini-skirt, black striped turtleneck, black tights, and high-heeled Mary Janes. The look was very funky and fresh.

"That looks better on you then it did on me," Eden complimented her.

"Hey, Eden! Buying a dress for the dance?"

"I'm trying to, but I can't find anything I like," she said as she hung up the dresses Claudia had tried on.

"Who are you going with?" Angie asked as she followed her.

"No one."

"You mean Dexter hasn't worked up his courage yet?"

"To do what?" Eden absently asked as she tried to hang a dress back on a crowded rack.

"Ask you to the dance!" Angie exclaimed.

Eden dropped the dresses she was holding and whirled around to face Angie. "What did you say?"

"Dexter wants to take you to the Valentine's Day dance."

"He does?" Eden asked in disbelief.

"All he ever talks about is you," Angie said.

Eden bent down to pick up the dresses she had dropped. "I thought *maybe* he might like me, but I wasn't sure. I thought I was imagining things."

"Oh, he likes you. Trust me. He likes you a lot. He's just too shy to do anything about it!" One of Angie's friends called out to her. "Gotta go!" she told Eden.

After Angie left, Eden went back to the dress racks with renewed determination. This time she was going to find a dress. If she didn't find one here, then she'd go to every store in the mall.

She had to.

Because it looked like she might have a date for the Valentine's Day dance after all!

ked in DeVille's, people
ntine's Day. The candy
vith shoppers waiting in
nimals and heart-shaped
he jewelry department
esclerks hurried to open
ney could take out shiny
d rings. Other shoppers
tucked under their arms.

t until the following day.
have a valentine.
wasn't a *real* valentine,

e, Jennifer had thought
he had made a decision.

She was going to tell Will how she felt about him. She had to. Once the Valentine's Day dance was over, they would no longer be a couple and she didn't want that to happen. She wanted to keep being Will's girlfriend, but for real. She could only hope that once she told him how she felt, he would tell her that he had feelings for her, too.

But he had to! She was sensing *something* developing between them. It couldn't be her imagination.

At that moment, the doors to the elevator across from Jennifer's cash register opened and Will came walking out. His overcoat was open and she could see he was wearing the suit they'd bought earlier in the week. He looked *so* good in it! Like he'd stepped out of the pages of a fashion magazine.

Jennifer's heart began beating nervously. Why was Will all dressed up and coming to see her? Was he planning to do something romantic? She walked out from behind her cash register. "Hi! This is a surprise."

"I swung by your house and your mom told me you were working. I wanted to talk to you about something."

"I wanted to talk to you about something,

too," Jennifer said, taking Will by the hand and leading him to the storeroom in the back. "Let's go where we can have some privacy." She was going to do it. She was going to tell him how she felt. If she didn't do it now, she might never do it.

"I can't stay away from my register very long," she said, as they stepped into a room filled with wedding gowns hanging in plastic bags. "Like I said, I wanted to talk to you about something, but I also wanted to give you something."

"What?"

"An early Valentine's Day present."

Then Jennifer threw her arms around Will and gave him a kiss. She'd been wanting to do this since the moment he'd ended their last kiss. And now she was.

But as she pressed her lips against Will's, she realized something was wrong.

This kiss wasn't as special as the last one they'd shared.

Maybe that was because Will wasn't kissing her back.

Jennifer broke the kiss and stepped away from Will, totally confused. Should she not have made the first move? Was Will upset about that? Was that why he hadn't kissed her back? She had expected a completely different reaction than the one she was getting. He was staring at her with an uncomfortable look on his face. Her kiss couldn't have been that bad, could it?

"Is something wrong?" she asked him.

Will quickly shook his head. "No, that was nice," he said. "Very nice."

"I wanted to thank you for being so sweet," she said, rushing to do damage control. After the way he'd responded to her kiss she wasn't about to confess her feelings. "You know, for helping me out."

"I'm always there for my friends. You know that better than anyone else. Which is what I wanted to talk to you about." Will paused and gazed down at the floor. It was almost like he was trying to work up his courage for what he had to say next. Then he gazed back at Jennifer. "That's why I dropped by last night," he continued. "But Violet was there and the timing didn't seem right. And today we never really had a chance to be alone."

He's breaking up with me, Jennifer thought. *He's decided he can't go through with this anymore.*

Wait, wait, wait! He can't *be breaking up with me because there's nothing to break up. We're not a couple.*

Her frantic thoughts must have registered on her face because Will laughed. "Don't look so panicked," he said. "It's not bad news."

"Then why are you acting so strangely?" Jennifer asked.

"Because I'm not sure how you're going to react when I tell you."

"Then just tell me," she told him. "The suspense is killing me!"

"Do you know Kristy Jenkins?"

Jennifer shook her head. The name rang no bells with her.

"She's a girl I went out with a couple of times. We're still friends. She goes to St. Bernadette's. Anyway, I ran into her on Sunday afternoon and she asked if I'd do her a favor."

"What kind of favor?"

"She has a party to go to tonight and she asked if I'd go with her. Her boyfriend broke up with her and she doesn't want to go alone. All her friends are coupled up."

"What did you tell her?"

"I said yes."

Jennifer couldn't believe what she was hearing. "You said yes? But why?"

"Why not?"

"Because you're supposed to be *my* boyfriend." She stared at Will in the suit she thought he had worn for her. But he hadn't. He was wearing it for another girl. And then she remembered helping him shop for it. She had asked him why he needed a suit and he hadn't told her. But he'd known that he needed the suit for tonight. Okay, he hadn't technically *lied*, but he'd withheld information from her! She'd thought she was dressing Will for herself, but she'd actually been dressing him for Kristy! "How is it going to look if people find out you're on a date with another girl? You know how everyone at North Ridge High gossips. All we need is for Mindy Yee to be at this party and we're sunk!"

"It will look like you trust me," Will said. "And it's not a *real* date. It's like what I'm doing for you by pretending to be your boyfriend. A favor. I'm helping a friend. It's the same thing."

Will's words rang through Jennifer's head: *Pretending to be your boyfriend . . . a favor . . .*

helping a friend. She'd just gotten a cold dose of reality. Will *didn't* have feelings for her. If he did, he wouldn't be saying those words. He'd be saying something else.

Something she wasn't ever going to get to hear from him.

Like: *I love you.*

Okay, maybe it was a bit too early for Will to be declaring his love, but at some point maybe he would have.

"Why are you freaking out?" Will asked, breaking into her thoughts. "I thought you'd be cool with it."

"Well, I'm not."

"Why? What's the big deal?"

Do you even have to ask that question? she wanted to scream. *Because I'm jealous!!! I don't want you spending time with another girl. I want you spending time with* me. *I know how great you are and Kristy Jenkins probably does, too. I wouldn't be surprised if she made a play for you!*

It's a big deal because I'm falling for you and I don't want to lose you. I don't want you going out with some other girl. I want you going out with me. Only me.

And then Jennifer remembered something that made her feel like an idiot. The necklace she had seen Will buying. She'd thought he was buying it for her, but he wasn't. Why would he? It wasn't the kind of Valentine's Day gift a guy would give to a girl who was "just" a friend. A guy gave a gift like that to a girl whom he cared about. That wasn't her. Will had made that perfectly clear.

So whom had he bought the necklace for?

Kristy Jenkins?

Or some other girl?

"I've got to get back to my register," Jennifer said, needing to get away from Will before she said something she'd regret. Part of her wanted to ask him whom he had bought the necklace for while another part of her wanted to scream and shout at him and ask why he hadn't bought the necklace for her. "Do whatever you need to do."

"Thanks," Will said, his voice filled with relief. "I'll see you at school tomorrow."

A feeling of sadness washed over Jennifer as she left the storeroom. She thought she had been special. She had thought she was the only girl who mattered to Will.

But she wasn't.

She never had been.

Violet had been right.

The Heartbreaker had succeeded in breaking her heart.

Chapter Nineteen

"Happy Valentine's Day!" Natalie exclaimed when Leo opened his front door the following morning.

Leo blinked at Natalie with sleepy eyes. "What are you doing here?"

"I'm taking you jogging. Weren't you waiting for me? You're wearing your sweats."

"That's 'cause I slept in them. My mom didn't have a chance to do the laundry last night and I didn't have any pajamas." Leo yawned. "I'm finished with jogging. I told you that yesterday."

Natalie walked into Leo's foyer and closed the front door behind her. "But you can't give up. I won't let you!"

Natalie followed after Leo as he headed back to his bedroom and flopped down on his bed. It was a typical guy room, with posters of bikini-clad girls on the walls, stacks of DVDs next to his computer, books and magazines scattered on the floor, and piles of discarded clothes everywhere.

"Go away," Leo mumbled, pulling the sheets and bedspread back over his head. "I need to sleep. If my parents hadn't already left for work, I'd make them throw you out."

Natalie shook her head. "It's time to rise and shine!"

Leo sighed and sat up. "Jogging around some park isn't going to help me lose weight."

"Yes, it will."

"No, it won't. Look, Nat, it's nice that you want to help me, but I'm not fooling myself. I'm always going to be fat."

"You're not," Natalie insisted. "Not if you want to lose the weight badly enough. Do you want to lose it?"

Leo ran a hand through his curls. "Of course I do!"

"Then why won't you try? What are you so afraid of?"

"What if I can't do it?" Leo whispered. "I've tried before. I've lost a few pounds but never enough to make a difference. And then I've put it back on."

"You *can* do it," Natalie said.

"Why do you sound so sure?"

"It's possible to lose the weight, Leo. I can prove it."

Natalie reached into her backpack and pulled out a photo album, placing it in Leo's lap. She'd never shown the album to anyone in North Ridge, but she trusted Leo. And she needed to do this. For him.

"What's this?" he asked.

"You tell me."

Leo began flipping through the pages of the photo album. "It's filled with pictures of some fat girl."

"You don't recognize her?"

Leo peered more closely at one of the photos. "Should I?"

"That fat girl is me."

Leo's mouth opened in shock as he stared at the photos before him and back at Natalie. Then he did it again. And again.

"That's you?" Leo gasped, pointing at a photo.

Natalie nodded. "That's me. Hard to believe, isn't it?"

Leo stared at the photos again. "I'll say. It's like you're two different people." He closed the album and stared at Natalie. His gaze was so intense that she started to squirm.

"What?" she asked, feeling self-conscious.

"Everything makes sense now. Why you've always been so nice to me. You used to *be* me."

"I knew what you were going through. And I'd like to think I still would have been nice to you, even if I hadn't been fat. I treat people the way I want them to treat me. With kindness and compassion."

Natalie then told Leo about her life before moving to North Ridge. It was the first time she had ever told the story to one of her new friends. As the words spilled out, she felt like a huge load was being lifted off her shoulders. It felt good sharing her secret. And if it helped Leo, even better.

"If I can do it, you can do it," she said when she finished. "I did it by myself, but I can help you, Leo."

"I don't think Tom would like that very much, do you?" Leo asked.

Tom. Natalie didn't want to think about him. He still wasn't talking to her after the way he'd blown up at her the day before. Even though she was his girlfriend, she didn't feel like one. A girlfriend was supposed to feel special. Wanted.

She'd never felt that way with Tom. When she was with him, she always felt like she was an accessory: the good-looking blonde that he needed to have on his arm.

Unlike Leo. He always made her feel special. He saw the person she was on the inside and not the outside.

"I didn't think so," Leo said when Natalie didn't answer.

"I don't care what Tom thinks," Natalie stated. "Want to know why?"

"Why?"

"I'm breaking up with him."

"How come?"

"I want to go out with someone else. Someone I like and who I think likes me."

"Another basketball player?"

"Nope."

"Football? Baseball?"

"Wrong again."

"Well, he must be a member of the jock squad, right?"

"Why would you think that?"

"Guys like that always date girls like you."

Natalie crooked a finger at Leo. "Come closer. I want to tell you a secret."

Leo leaned into Natalie.

"Sometimes girls like me date guys like *you*," she whispered into his ear.

Leo pulled back, staring at Natalie in shock. She slowly nodded and then she caught him off guard by throwing her arms around him and pulling him close as she gave him a kiss.

"Wow," a dazed Leo said when the kiss ended.

"I've been wanting to do that ever since you kissed me yesterday morning," Natalie said, seconds before she started to give Leo a second kiss. "Guess you're not the only one with no willpower!"

Eden was dressed to impress.

Last night she had spent hours in front of her closet searching for the perfect outfit to wear today. It needed to be something that made Dexter notice her more than he had in the past. She finally decided on a black mini skirt — the better to show off her legs! — with a purple camisole top paired with a cropped jacket and black high-heeled boots. She'd gotten up extra early that morning, taking time with her hair and makeup, because she wanted to look *gorgeous*. And she did! Beyoncé had better watch out!

Eden still couldn't believe that Dexter liked her. If she hadn't run into Angie yesterday, she still wouldn't know. Why hadn't she been able to see it for herself? In the past, she had always known when a guy was interested in her. But usually those guys were jocks or they hung out with her crowd of friends. She could read the signals. She and Dexter, though, came from two different worlds. He was super smart and she was super popular. The two didn't usually go together. Maybe that was why she hadn't known. Because it had never occurred to her. And maybe the reason why Dexter had never asked her out was that he didn't think she'd *want* to go out with him. But why wouldn't she? He was sweet and kind and one of the smartest guys at North Ridge High.

She saw Dexter walk into the library and waved to him. Cradled under his arm was a package wrapped with silver foil paper decorated with red hearts. That sweetie! He'd gotten her a Valentine's Day present!

"Hi, Dexter," she said when he reached the table. She had made sure her chair was pushed away from the table, legs casually crossed, so he could see what she was wearing from head to toe. She wanted him to notice the entire package.

"Hi, Eden."

Much to her disappointment, he didn't even glance at her. He just dropped his package on the table and started unloading his book bag, his eyes focused downward.

Hmmm. He hadn't commented on what she was wearing. *Very* strange. This outfit had gotten her results on more than one occasion. She *knew* it worked. Of course, Dexter *was* shy. That's probably why he wasn't saying anything.

"Whatcha got there?" she nonchalantly asked, pointing to the package on the table.

He shrugged. "I don't know. I found it in front of my locker this morning."

That wasn't the answer Eden had been expecting. "It's a present for *you*?" she choked out.

Dexter nodded, showing Eden the card that had been addressed to him. His name was on it, but that was all. "Looks like I have a secret admirer."

Hearing those words, Eden instantly became jealous.

Someone else was interested in *her* Dexter?

"Aren't you going to open it up?" she asked.

"I'll do it later," Dexter said, sitting down and flipping through his SAT study guide. "We've got work to do!"

But Eden didn't want to study. She wanted Dexter to unwrap that package! *Now!* She needed to know what she was up against. She hadn't planned on dealing with any competition.

Was she going to lose Dexter before she even had him?

Chapter Twenty

Jennifer was down in the dumps.

It was Valentine's Day, and everywhere she turned at North Ridge High, couples were celebrating the day. They were hugging and kissing and giving each other red-and-pink-wrapped gifts. Boxes of chocolate were being passed around and she kept hearing shouts of "Happy Valentine's Day!"

Jennifer maneuvered through the crowded hallway on the way to her locker. She tried to block out everything that was going on around her. She didn't want to be reminded that, once again, she had no valentine.

She hadn't cried herself to sleep the night before, but she'd come close. As she lay in bed, twisting and turning against the sheets, she kept thinking of Will and Kristy. What had they done that night? Even though they were only "friends," had their night together reignited things between them? Had Will taken Kristy home and walked her to her front door? Had he kissed her good night? Had they made plans to get together again? Because after tonight, Will could go out with whomever he wanted.

While she would be all alone.

Jennifer had finally dozed off after midnight but she kept waking up throughout the night. She was so restless that Sheba, who usually slept at the foot of her bed, had jumped off and left her bedroom to find someplace else to sleep.

"What's with the sad face?" Violet asked as Jennifer reached her locker. Their lockers were side by side and Violet's was already open.

"I'm not sad," Jennifer said.

"Yes, you are." Violet took a closer look at Jennifer. "In fact, you look like you're depressed."

"I'm not depressed."

"You could have fooled me. Are you sure everything is okay?"

Jennifer began fiddling with the combination of her lock. "I don't want to talk about it."

Even though Violet was her best friend and she wasn't the type to say "I told you so," Jennifer couldn't tell her what had happened with Will the night before or why it hurt so much. It was too embarrassing.

"That means there *is* something wrong."

"Just let it go, Violet, please?" Jennifer's lock clicked open and she pulled it off. Seconds later, when she opened her locker door, a cascade of red, pink, peach, yellow, lilac, and white rose petals flooded out.

"Oh my gosh!" Violet squealed.

Jennifer stepped away from her locker in disbelief as the petals kept pouring out. It was like a rainbow of colors!

"Who could have done this?" a stunned Jennifer asked.

"That's a silly question!" Violet exclaimed, pointing to the note taped to the inside of Jennifer's locker door. "Will! Your valentine!"

The note card was pink. Scrawled in Will's distinct handwriting was: *Happy Valentine's Day, Red! I wanted to give you roses, but I didn't want you pricking your fingers on any thorns so I figured I'd just give you the petals. I also couldn't make up my mind on what color to send, in case you hadn't noticed.*

"This is *so* romantic," Violet said as she scooped up a handful of petals and let them drift back onto the pile. "You can use these to make potpourri."

By then, a bunch of girls had gathered around Jennifer, oohing and aahing over Will's gift.

Even though Jennifer was smiling on the outside, inside she wasn't. Will had left the rose petals because of the Most Romantic Couple contest. He was doing it because they were pretending. It wasn't like he cared about her.

"Hey!" a passing Mindy Yee exclaimed. "Claudia and Chase just pulled up in front of the school in a pink horse-drawn sleigh!"

The other girls left the pile of rose petals and hurried after Mindy.

"Looks like Claudia trumps me again," Jennifer sighed.

"Temporarily," Violet said. "There's still tonight, when the Most Romantic Couple is going to be announced. That's the big prize."

But what does it matter? Jennifer wondered. Even if she and Will did win, it wasn't like it was going to mean anything. They weren't a couple. They never were and they never would be.

* * *

At lunchtime, the votes were being cast. Jennifer had no idea who was going to win. From the conversations she'd overheard, it sounded like every couple had their supporters.

After voting for herself and Will, Jennifer joined Violet at their table. She was squirting some ketchup over her fries when Claudia came over, holding out a cell phone.

"The game's over," she triumphantly announced.

Jennifer licked some ketchup off her fingers. "What are you talking about?"

"Take a look at this photo," Claudia said, handing over the phone. "It was taken last night."

Jennifer stared at the photo. It was Will and another girl. He was wearing the suit he had bought at DeVille's. That meant the girl had to be Kristy Jenkins. Jennifer looked back up at Claudia. "So?"

"I was checking out wedding halls with my sister Pam, and while we were there, a party was going on in one of the ballrooms. Imagine how surprised I was when I peeked inside and saw Will with another girl, especially when she introduced Will as her *date* to her friends! Why would

Will be with another girl if he's *so* into you? Unless he's *not* and the two of you have been pretending to be a couple this entire time!"

Jennifer laughed. "That girl is Kristy Jenkins. She goes to St. Bernadette's. She and Will used to date. He took her out last night as a favor. I knew all about it."

Jennifer was about to hand the cell phone back to Claudia when she noticed something. How had she missed it? There was a necklace around Kristy's neck. It was the same necklace she saw Will buying at Bring the Bling yesterday afternoon. Now she knew whom he was buying it for.

Kristy.

Claudia snatched her cell phone out of Jennifer's hand and stormed back to her table.

"What's the matter?" Violet asked after Claudia left. "You look like you've seen a ghost."

Jennifer shook her head. She couldn't talk. If she tried, she was going to lose it. All she kept seeing was that necklace. Will had bought it for Kristy and he'd given it to her last night. In her mind, she saw Will standing behind Kristy, placing the necklace around her neck. It had probably been a Valentine's Day gift. That's what a guy did when he cared about a girl: he gave her a gift to show her how he felt. To let her know how special she was to him.

She'd known the necklace wasn't for her. She'd figured that out last night.

So why did it hurt so much now that she knew for sure?

"I thought I had her this time!" Claudia exclaimed as she returned to her table and plopped back down in her seat between Natalie and Eden.

"What are you complaining about now?" Natalie asked as she sipped a Diet Pepsi.

"Jennifer!" Claudia scratched her arm. "I thought I had proof that she and Will had been scamming everybody, but they weren't."

"Can't you let it go?" Natalie asked. She was *so* over the Claudia-Jennifer feud, especially since she thought Jennifer was nice. "Will and Jennifer are a couple whether you like it or not. A very cute couple, if you want my opinion."

"I don't!" Claudia snapped as she began furiously scratching her other arm.

"Did someone sprinkle you with itching powder?" Eden asked.

"I've been scratching myself all morning!" Claudia complained. "Maybe it's this new sweater I'm wearing."

Natalie decided to drop a bombshell. She didn't know any other way to do it, other than asking, and she needed some advice. "How awful is it to break up with a guy on Valentine's Day?"

Eden's mouth dropped open. "You're breaking up with Tom?"

Natalie nodded. "There's someone else and I want to be with him tonight, not Tom. I'm sure Tom'll be able to find someone to go to the dance with him. He's never had any trouble getting a date."

"But you're running for Most Romantic Couple," Eden reminded her. "Isn't it going to look strange to have one of the competing couples show up with other dates?"

"We were never going to win. And we were never romantic to begin with. Tom entered us in the contest because he was competing with Chase, that's all. And I don't care how it looks. I don't want to be with Tom. I want to be with this other guy."

Natalie thought back to that morning after she'd kissed Leo. She'd told him again that she was breaking up with Tom because she wanted to be with him. Leo hadn't been able to believe it.

"Why not?" she had asked him. "I like you. I want to go out with you. Not Tom. Don't you want to go out with me?"

"Of course!"

She had gazed around the bedroom at his discarded piles of clothes. "Then you better find a suit somewhere in these piles, because you're taking me to the Valentine's Day dance tonight!"

"If Tom was more into another girl, he wouldn't hesitate to dump you," Eden said. "Trust me, I've been there. Learn from my experience! I say if you're interested in this other guy, then go for it!"

"Absolutely," Claudia agreed as she began scratching her back. "Are you trading up?"

"If you mean am I going out with a guy who cares about me, yes," Natalie answered.

"Who is it?" Eden asked.

"Leo Barnes."

Claudia stopped scratching. *"Blubber Boy?"* she gasped. "You're dumping a hottie like Tom Marland for that fat blob? Have you gone crazy?"

Natalie's temper snapped. "Don't you *ever* call Leo by that horrible nickname again! You don't know anything about Leo. Maybe if you talked to him, you would."

"I'm in two classes with Leo," Eden said. "He seems like a nice guy."

"He is. And he's taking me to the dance tonight."

Claudia rolled her eyes. "No comment." She turned to Eden. "Have you found a date or will you be going solo?"

Eden chewed on her lower lip. "Well, there *is* someone I'd like to go to the dance with, but I think another girl is interested in him. I don't know what to do."

"What are you waiting for?" Natalie asked. "Make your move!"

"Who is it?" Claudia asked as she began scratching again.

"Dexter King," Eden said.

"Your nerdy tutor?" Claudia exclaimed, eyes widening with horror. "I can't believe what I'm hearing! Why do the two of you want to date those losers?"

Natalie pushed herself away from the table. She'd finally had enough of Claudia. It was time

ey're *not* losers. Not to us.
s all that matters."
idge them?" Eden asked,

ate losers," Claudia stated
they do, they're *not* my

clear. But Natalie didn't
n I guess you're going to
friends," she said, tossing
shoulder.
en added.
" Claudia hissed. "You're
d Dexter!"
f using the word *loser,*
. "You and Chase haven't
mantic Couple yet. You
t firsthand later tonight
s." She peered closely at
n case you didn't know it,
k out. You've got a bunch
d."
e table with Eden behind
Claudia, still scratching,
er shoulder bag to find a
check out her face.

Chapter Twenty-One

"I figured I'd save you the trouble of tracking me down," Tom said.

Classes had ended for the day and Tom was leaning against Natalie's locker. The hallways had cleared out and the school was pretty much deserted. With the exception of a few stragglers, most students had left to start getting ready for the Valentine's Day dance.

Finding Tom waiting for her was an unpleasant surprise. He'd caught her off guard even though she'd been planning to track him down before going home. She hadn't seen him the entire day and she hadn't wanted to break up with him over the phone. She wanted to do it in person. Hopefully Tom would understand why she was doing it. She didn't want to hurt his

ed to do was tell him

was looking for you?"

ted, trying to remember
epared earlier. But her

om pretended to think.
ngers. "You're not going

ain —"
ou can save your speech.
me in. She told me all

done that," Natalie said,
prised. Getting even was

waited until tomorrow to
e's Day! We're competing
ple."
uple!" Natalie exclaimed.
couple. We were hardly
friend. Our being in that
only entered us because
th Chase."
ie's words. "What about

"What about it?"

"We were supposed to go together."

"You never asked me to the dance," Natalie told him.

"Yes, I did."

"No, you didn't. You just assumed because we were dating that we were going together. Just like everything else. You always called the shots. You never consulted with me on anything. You expected me to go along with everything you decided."

"So you're dumping me because I never let you pick a movie?"

"No!" she exclaimed in frustration. "You don't get it, do you? You liked the way I looked and that was about it. You never liked *me*, the person I was on the inside, because you never bothered to get to know me. Why do you think we did so lousy on that romance test yesterday?"

"Does Leo *know* you?" Tom sneered.

"Yes, he does," Natalie said. "He knows everything about me."

Tom pushed himself away from Natalie's locker. He stared at her from head to toe and then shook his head in disgust. "You better make sure to take a picture of yourself and then save it."

ıtand what Tom was say-

ɔt going to look like
e you start dating Leo,
ꞓ as fat as he is. Then
ɫ have Blubber Boy and

ɪ react to Tom's words,
ıg by her head.
m's face.
ɔped open in shock as an
off Tom's face, leaving
ed cream, chocolate pud-
aham cracker crust. She
ʼ a sheepish Leo.
ne Ec for Bonnie," he
ıg to Lisa last night and
't feeling too well. She's
nething. I was going to
ınd I came to see if you
ıt then I heard what Tom
gged. "Even though I'm
couldn't let him talk that

d a finger in Leo's face.
nething like that again!"

"I won't," a contrite Leo promised as a sputtering Tom wiped off his face.

"Because you've wasted a perfectly good dessert!" Natalie laughed, hooking her arm through Leo's and walking away from Tom. "Now we need to find ourselves another chocolate cream pie. Only we're going to eat this one!"

Eden stood in front of Dexter's house, her feet frozen in place.

She couldn't move.

All she had to do was walk to the front door and ring the doorbell. Then when Dexter answered the door, she'd ask him if he wanted to go to the Valentine's Day dance with her. Easy enough.

So why couldn't she do it?

What was she so afraid of?

The answer came immediately.

Rejection.

Even though Angie had told her that Dexter liked her, she was afraid of showing him her feelings. Whenever she'd shown a guy her feelings, he'd hurt her, and she didn't want to be hurt again. But somebody needed to make the first move. If she didn't, who knew when Dexter

nted to. There was still
al with. She might make
er.

you? What are you

and found herself fac-
He was holding a bunch
balloons that said BE
ing the balloons weren't

our secret admirer?" she
and jealous and wishing
alloon.

rds out while keeping a
must really like you."
ness."

already? I'm supposed to
Not her! Is sending you a
you to fall for someone? If
at my father's credit card!
ing here?" Dexter asked

led, trying to make up a
Why hadn't she thought

She held out her wrist, showing off a silver charm bracelet. "I lost one of my charms and I think it might have fallen off when I was over on Saturday night. Do you mind if I look for it?"

"Come on in," Dexter said as he searched his jacket pocket for his house keys.

Once inside, Dexter headed up to his bedroom with the balloons while Eden pretended to search the living room. What did she do now? There was no missing charm. She hadn't even been wearing the bracelet on Saturday night! Luckily, Dexter hadn't remembered. Now all she had to do was work up the courage to ask him to the dance by the time he came back.

"Find it?" Dexter asked when he came back downstairs.

Eden jumped from the couch cushion she was flipping over. He was back already? She saw he had changed into a pair of sweatpants and a long-sleeved T-shirt. "I must have lost it somewhere else. Sorry to have bothered you. I better go. I'm sure you've got lots of homework to do."

Dexter walked her to the front door. "Is everything okay, Eden? You seem kind of jumpy. Jittery."

That's because I don't know how to ask you to the dance!

competition!

Eden tippy-toed to the kitchen door, pressing her ear against it. It was hard to hear the conversation on the other side, but from what little she could hear, Dexter was laughing. Laughing! Girls always tried to make guys laugh when they were flirting with them. That could only mean one thing. He was talking to *her*!

She needed to know what she was up against. Eden pressed her ear more closely against the door, wanting to hear things more clearly. As she did, the door unexpectedly swung inward and she fell to the kitchen floor, flat on her stomach, right at Dexter's feet. He stared down at her in shock.

"I'll have to call you back," he said, hanging up the phone and returning to Eden as she struggled to stand up.

"Are you okay?" he asked, helping her to her feet.

Eden was totally embarrassed. What did Dexter think of her?

"What were you doing?"

Eden couldn't take the suspense any longer. She had to know. "Were you talking with her?"

"Her?"

"You know. Your secret admirer. The one who's trying to take you away from me!" she blurted out.

"Take me away from you? Eden, are you feeling okay?" Dexter stared at her with concern. "Did you hit your head when you fell? You're not making any sense."

Eden knew actions spoke louder than words. So instead of answering Dexter's questions, she threw her arms around him and gave him a kiss.

"What was that for?" a stunned Dexter asked when Eden pulled her lips away from his.

"I'm crazy about you, Dexter King. I don't know why it took me so long to realize it. You're sweet and you're smart and you're thoughtful and any girl would be lucky to go out with you." Eden paused and then exclaimed, "I want to be that girl! Will you be my date for the Valentine's Day dance? That is, if you don't already have a date."

"Who would I go with?" Dexter asked.

"Your secret admirer."

"I don't even know who she is."

"Weren't you just talking to her on the phone?"

"I was talking to my friend Ozzy."

"So you don't know who's been crushing on you?"

"I don't know and I don't care." Dexter closed the distance between himself and Eden, lifting a hand to her cheek. "Want to know why?"

"Why?"

He leaned forward and whispered in her ear. "Because you're the only girl for me."

"I am?" Eden asked in disbelief.

Dexter nodded.

"I am!" Eden happily shouted.

At that moment, Angie, Yvonne, and Thelma burst into the kitchen.

"Yay!" they exclaimed. "It worked! It worked!"

"What's going on?" a confused Eden asked as Dexter's sisters danced around them. "What worked?"

"Our plan!" Yvonne exclaimed.

"What plan?" Dexter asked, sounding just as confused as Eden.

"*We're* your secret admirer," Angie confessed.

"It was us!" Yvonne cried. "Us! Us! Us!"

"We wanted to make Eden jealous and it worked," Thelma said.

"Somebody had to get the two of you together. Otherwise you'd still be pining away for each other," Angie explained. "After I told Eden that you were crazy about her, I decided she needed a little push. When a girl knows that another girl is interested in her guy, she'll do whatever it takes to snag him."

"We sent you those gifts," Thelma explained.

"I picked out the balloons!" Yvonne shouted.

Eden couldn't believe Dexter's sisters had been so sneaky. Luckily, she had played right into their hands!

"Listen to your little sisters, Dexter," Eden said. "They *so* know how the female mind works!"

Chapter Twenty-Two

When Jennifer got home from school, she found a package waiting on her doorstep. It was a square box wrapped in red foil with a pink bow on it. The card attached had her name on it.

She instantly recognized the handwriting.

It was Will's.

Another fake Valentine's Day present.

She snatched up the box and brought it inside, shaking it against her ear. It didn't make a sound, but she wasn't the least bit curious about what was inside. Why should she care? The gift didn't mean anything. Just like the rose petals hadn't meant anything. It was all for show.

After hanging up her coat, Jennifer tossed the box on the couch in the living room and headed into the kitchen. There she found Sheba sitting in front of the sliding glass doors. Outside, on the other side of the glass, was a yowling tomcat missing one eye.

"Even you have a valentine!" Jennifer told her cat.

After grabbing a handful of Oreos, Jennifer went upstairs to her bedroom. She hadn't found a dress the day before, so she needed to search through her closet. It didn't matter what she wore, though. Will wasn't going to notice.

Flipping through her hangers, Jennifer pulled out an emerald green satin silk dress with spaghetti straps. She'd only worn it once, to her cousin Julia's wedding in November. When she bought the dress, her mom said that the color went perfect with her hair and skin tone and she'd been right. She'd gotten tons of compliments at the wedding.

Now that she knew what she was going to wear, she had to decide on how to do her hair. Up or down? If she wore it up, like she had at the wedding, she'd look more sophisticated. If she wore it down, she'd look hotter.

Definitely down.

She was putting the finishing touches on her makeup when the doorbell rang. That had

"You don't have to do that," she said as she closed the door behind him.

"Do what?"

"Pretend like you're interested. No one's watching."

"I wasn't pretending."

Jennifer walked past Will to get her coat out of the hall closet. "Whatever."

Will touched Jennifer's arm. "Are you mad at me?"

Jennifer casually stepped away from Will so his hand would fall off. She didn't want him touching her because she liked when he touched her. After tonight, there would be no more touching. She had to start getting used to it. "Why would I be mad?"

"You tell me," Will said. "This isn't about Kristy, is it?"

Jennifer laughed. "Kristy? I haven't thought about her at all," she lied.

Will placed a hand on Jennifer's shoulder, turning her around. He studied her from head to toe. "You look really pretty, but something's missing."

"Missing?"

"You didn't open up the gift I left for you."

Jennifer had forgotten all about it. She dropped her coat on a chair and went into the living room to retrieve Will's gift. When she returned to the front hall, she found Sheba meowing and rubbing herself against Will's legs. Traitor!

"She likes me," Will said, petting Sheba on the head.

"All the girls like you," Jennifer said as she tore away the wrapping paper on the box. When she lifted back the lid of the box, she gasped. She couldn't believe what she was seeing. Nestled against a bed of black velvet was a necklace with a heart-shaped pendant.

The same necklace she saw Will buying yesterday.

But he had bought it for Kristy Jenkins, hadn't he? She'd seen Kristy wearing this necklace in

·. What was

hing?" Will
it?"
;e?" Jennifer
›ercent off?"
;ked. "What

ı Will's face.
·terday after-
risty Jenkins

showing me
I saw it on

isty, I bought

ced.
nper starting
picious?"
Heartbreaker,

: on Sunday
cklace," Will
so I asked her

Jennifer hadn't expected to hear that. If he hadn't bought the necklace for Kristy, then that meant . . .

"You bought the necklace for me?" she squeaked, all her anger draining away. "Only me?"

"Uh-huh." Will took the necklace out of the box and stepped behind Jennifer, fastening it around her neck. "You never know when you're going to need to buy a present for someone special."

"Someone special?" she asked in disbelief.

"I don't know how you did it, Red, but you've gotten under my skin," Will whispered into her ear. "You drive me crazy! But you also make me laugh and smile and I can't remember the last time I had so much fun hanging out with someone. I don't want it to end after tonight."

Jennifer wanted to pinch herself. Was she dreaming? This couldn't be real, could it? Will was telling her the words she'd been longing to hear!

"You don't?" She turned around, gazing up at Will from between lowered lashes.

Will shook his head. "I don't. What do you say we try this for real?"

d answer, Will pulled her
her a kiss. It was a long,
as just as wonderful as
her. It was the perfect

oing out with me?" Will
ed. "Will you be my girl-

hed, giving Will a hug.
ne thing."

d!"

Chapter Twenty-Three

"Where's Claudia?" Eden asked Natalie as they stood on the dance floor of the auditorium and waited for Principal Hicks to announce which couple had been voted Most Romantic. "I haven't seen her all night. This is the moment she's been waiting for."

"Don't know and don't care," Natalie said as she held Leo's hand. There had been some stares when they'd arrived together but then they had ended. Not that the stares had bothered her. She didn't care what anyone said. All that mattered was being with Leo.

Mindy Yee, who was standing behind Eden and Natalie, stuck her head between them. "Didn't you hear?"

"Hear what?" Natalie asked.

"You mean you don't know?" Mindy gasped, a look of glee washing over her face as she got ready to drop her bombshell. "Claudia's got chicken pox!"

"No wonder she was scratching like crazy at lunch!" Eden exclaimed.

"No one knows where she could have gotten it," Mindy said. "Little kids usually get it and I can't see Claudia hanging out with little kids."

Natalie locked eyes with Leo. They knew exactly where Claudia had gotten the chicken pox. From Bonnie. Because like Claudia, Bonnie also had them. They had found out when they had visited her that afternoon.

"She's home in bed covered with pink calamine lotion," Mindy said. "I went to see her on my way to the dance. She was *not* happy."

But it serves her right for being so mean! Natalie wanted to say. *What goes around comes around.*

Eden giggled, clasping a hand over her mouth. Then she started to laugh.

"What's so funny?" Mindy asked.

"Claudia said she wanted to wear pink for Valentine's Day," Eden chuckled. "And now she is!"

* * *

"And the winners for Most Romantic Couple are . . ."

"Think we're going to win?" Will asked Jennifer as they waited to hear which couple's name would be announced.

"I don't know. And it really doesn't matter to me."

"Why's that?"

Jennifer snuggled closer to Will. "Because I got exactly what I wanted for Valentine's Day."

"Maybe we'll be competing as Most Romantic next year," Dexter whispered to Eden as they watched Principal Hicks open the sealed envelope in his hand.

"And the winners are Celia Armstrong and Freddy Keenan!" he announced. Applause broke out as Celia and Freddy walked to the front of the auditorium.

"You think we'll still be together a year from now?" Eden asked Dexter as everyone stepped off to the sides so Celia and Freddy could have the dance floor all to themselves.

A romantic song began as they started dancing.

"Are you ready to break up with me already?" Dexter joked.

"Of course not! I just don't need someone else telling me if my boyfriend is romantic," Eden said, thinking of the bouquet of pink roses and box of chocolates Dexter had given her when he'd come to pick her up that night. "My opinion is the only one that matters."

"So how am I doing so far?" Dexter asked, leading Eden onto the dance floor as other couples began joining Celia and Freddy.

"I want you to be mine," Eden said as she stepped into his arms and gave him a kiss. "All mine."

"Did you think you'd be dancing with me on Valentine's Day?" Leo asked Natalie.

It was a slow dance and their bodies were close together, Natalie resting her head on Leo's shoulder. She loved the way she felt in his arms. All warm and cozy.

"I didn't," Natalie said. "But now that I am, I wouldn't want to be anywhere else."

"Did I tell you how great you look?"

"A couple of times." Natalie was wearing a gold sequined minidress with puffed sleeves and gold high-heeled sandals. From her ears, she wore a pair of dangling gold leaf earrings. "You look pretty spiffy in your suit."

"I still can't believe we're here together." Leo stared down at the floor. "I never thought I'd have someone to be mine."

Natalie placed her hand under Leo's chin, lifting his head up. She looked deep into his eyes. "Believe it."

And then to prove it, she gave him a kiss.

When there was a break between songs, Jennifer raced over to Violet's side. She'd texted her earlier to tell her that she and Will were dating for real, but Violet hadn't said anything about the latest developments in her own love life. "*Who* is that hunk you're with? Have you been holding out on me? I want details and I want them *now*! You didn't tell me you were coming to the dance and you *didn't* tell me you'd be bringing a date!"

Violet giggled, her blue eyes gleaming with mischief behind her glasses. "That's Gino. He works at Marinelli's with Will."

"Where did you meet him?"

"Last night I ordered a pizza, and when Gino delivered it, I asked him if he wanted to come with me to the dance. I figured I'd take a page out of your book. What did I have to lose? He said yes! Who knows? If it worked for you, it might work for me!"

The music started again. "Gotta go!" Violet said as she hurried back out onto the dance floor and Gino. "Talk to you later!"

As Jennifer watched Violet and Gino start dancing to a slow song, Will came by her side.

"Feel like another dance?"

Jennifer couldn't get enough of being with Will. She wanted to dance with him all night. She took him by the hand and walked back out onto the dance floor.

"I wish this night would never end!" she exclaimed as she wrapped her arms around Will's neck and leaned into him.

"Having a good time?"

"The best!"

"Can I ask you a question, Jennifer?"

She looked at Will in surprise. "I think that's the first time you've called me by my name. Usually I'm Red."

"That's only when I'm trying to push your buttons. I know it drives you crazy."

"And now?"

"I'm being serious."

"I kind of like it when you call me Red," Jennifer confessed. "Even if I act like I don't. It makes me feel special." She gazed up at Will. "So what did you want to ask me?"

"Be mine?"

"Only if you promise to be mine."

Will pretended to think about it before giving Jennifer a smile. "Deal!" he exclaimed.

And then he sealed it with a kiss.

Take another trip to North Ridge High in

Secret Santa

By Sabrina James

Noelle focused her attention on the red velvet bag Mindy was holding. Then she dipped her hand inside, swirling it around the many slips of paper.

Somewhere inside was Charlie's name.

Unless it had already been picked.

Think positive! Noelle scolded herself. *Positive. Positive. Positive. Charlie's name is in this bag. It is! It is! It is! And I will pull it out. I will! I will! I will!*

Holding her breath, Noelle closed her eyes and reached into the very bottom of the bag, wrapped her fingers around a slip of paper, and pulled it out.

To Do List: Read all the Point books!

Airhead
By **Meg Cabot**

Suite Scarlett
By **Maureen Johnson**

The Year My Sister Got Lucky
South Beach
French Kiss
Hollywood Hills
By **Aimee Friedman**

The Heartbreakers
The Crushes
By **Pamela Wells**

This Book Isn't Fat, It's Fabulous
By **Nina Beck**

Wherever Nina Lies
By **Lynn Weingarten**

Summer Boys
By Hailey Abbott
Summer Boys
Next Summer
After Summer
Last Summer

In or Out
By Claudia Gabel
In or Out
Loves Me, Loves Me Not
Sweet and Vicious
Friends Close, Enemies Closer

Hotlanta
By Denene Millner and Mitzi Miller
Hotlanta
If Only You Knew
What Goes Around

Pool Boys
Meet Me at the Boardwalk
By **Erin Haft**

Popular Vote
By **Micol Ostow**

Top 8
By **Katie Finn**

Kissing Booth
By **Lexie Hill**

Love in the Corner Pocket
By **Marlene Perez**

Kissing Snowflakes
By **Abby Sher**

Orange Is the New Pink
By **Nina Malkin**

Once Upon a Prom
By Jeanine Le Ny
Dream
Dress
Date

I Heart Bikinis
He's With Me
By Tamara Summers
Island Summer
By Jeanine Le Ny
What's Hot
By Caitlyn Davis

Making a Splash
By Jade Parker
Robyn
Caitlin
Whitney

Secret Santa
Be Mine
By Sabrina James

To Catch A Pirate
By Jade Parker

21 Proms
Edited by **Daniel Ehrenhaft**
and **David Levithan**

www.thisispoint.com